RIVERS

OF

SILVER

RIVERS

OF

SILVER

David Bissenden

Troubador Publishing Ltd
Unit E2 Airfield Business Park,
Harrison Road, Market Harborough,
Leicestershire. LE16 7UL
Tel: 0116 2792299
Email: books@troubador.co.uk
Web: www.troubador.co.uk

ISBN 978 1836281 634

British Library Cataloguing in Publication Data.
A catalogue record for this book is available from the British Library.

Printed and bound in Great Britain by 4edge Limited
Typeset in 11pt Adobe Garamond Pro by Troubador Publishing Ltd, Leicester, UK

Dedicated to: Jane, Faith, Jon, Oliver, Dylan and Aria.

Sierra de la Ventana

It was Christmas Eve, the 24th December, 1868 and for this year, as for the previous three, the Hope family would be spending it a long way from their homeland.

Joyce Hope, her four-year-old son Fontaine and husband George lived in a cottage or what the Spanish might call a hacienda – in the village of Sierra de la Ventana in the foothills of the mountain range which boasted the same name. From the outside the house looked like a typical Argentine hacienda, single-storied with white stucco walls and red tile roof; but inside it was a little piece of England, dropped here on the western edge of the Argentine pampas. It had all the trappings of a fine colonial house with a morning room, parlour, library and large room at the back for the two servants – Rosina and her mother Maria – to prepare food. The whole house had the air of a middle-class residence in the English Home Counties. Joyce had done everything to make it comfortable and homely. A nice garden, full of English flowers, Acacia shrubs and Mimosa trees. Inside, they ate on white linen tablecloths using silver cutlery and willow-patterned bone china crockery. Even the furniture – bought from the best dealers in Buenos Aires – would not have looked out of place in an English country house in Essex, which was their original home.

Joyce was in the house all day and spent much of her time sitting beside the window in the morning room from where she looked out over the garden – now full of English roses and early flowering shrubs, across the fast-flowing Rio Sauce Grande, to the never-ending vista of the flat pampas beyond. She was particularly assiduous in keeping the house tidy and attractive today as her husband, George, had gone to Bahia Blanca on the coast, thirty miles distant, to collect the payroll from the Bank of the Province of Buenos Aires. He was now riding back, with an armed escort, and was due back soon.

On the other side of the morning room was her four-year-old boy Fontaine playing on his beloved wooden rocking horse. He was watched over studiously by his nanny, Rosina, a girl of similar age to Joyce – early thirties. Rosina also had a child, a son Frederico, who was only three years old. Of course Fontaine did not regard riding the rocking horse as just play. No, he was in training to get a real horse and be a real rider, like the gauchos who worked on his father's ranch. A real cowboy with spurs and guns and everything. Rosina and Joyce both looked on at his earnest efforts to ride the rocking horse and smiled. He could not wait to grow up and be like his father.

Meanwhile, only a few miles' distant George Hope had had more than enough of riding for the day. He was heading across the featureless pampas, heading home to Ventana and his beloved family. It had been tiresome, this thirty-mile ride on horseback from the scruffy seaport of Bahia Blanca back to his home. It was midsummer too, and hot and dusty – thankless weather for riders and horses. The sky was cloudless and the heat was causing beads of sweat to glisten on his forehead. One day, he hoped, a railway would be put through here, but for now this gravel road, which linked the coast to the village, was the only real option. To safeguard the wages he had employed a troop of nine men; himself and Pedro his foreman from the ranch, and seven officers from the local uniformed Guardia who were laden with guns, swords, and all manner of equipment. Despite this, the Guardia gave an impression that they were pretty raw and probably not going to be much good in a real fight. Even their grey uniforms looked to be badly fitting, like the costumes in a bad play... Perhaps though their very presence might deter the bandits, who, let's face it, could appear from anywhere, at any time. Normally the payroll convoy would have gone to the estancia, the ranch itself, and the wages would be allotted in the office there, but this week the air was full of rumours of dissident gauchos, roaming the southern pampas looking for anything they could rob. George hated how some of these, once noble, horsemen had become virtual outlaws, living outside normal society and preying on the ranch owners who were bringing wealth to this new country. Some had worked for him in the past, and their skills herding and splitting the cattle were second to none. As long as they were paid and kept in yerba mate – their favourite tea drink – they had seemed content. Sure they were always brandishing their precious knives, known as facons, and making sure everyone knew they were not to be messed with. But surely that was mostly bravado. Times were changing. George felt sad at this, one of the reasons he had come to the Argentine was because the country was so new, so fresh. There was land for the taking, endless possibilities compared with back in Essex where every square yard of land was owned by someone else and locked up by deeds and history, aristocrats owning more land than the eye could see, just because their forefathers had taken it centuries back. That is why this new world seemed so inviting, so full of possibilities, they could write their own laws, plan their own future in this wild land where the flat pampas stretched to far distant horizons...

But with opportunity came danger. This threat of the unknown was never clearer than in the behaviour of some of the gauchos. Their roving lifestyle was under threat from the ranch owners and agents of the government who were fencing off land, making effortless riding harder, and casual work more difficult to find. So some had gone rogue, becoming true bandits and were now living a nomadic existence outside the law. One day these lands would be under control, but for now they sometimes resembled the Wild West, with cattle rustling and people taking the law into their own hands. It had been a culture shock for George when he first came here but now he knew the score.

Reluctantly he had agreed to take the payroll back to his home in the foothills which had better natural defences than the estancia on the open pampas. His house also had a river running between it and the pampas, with only one crossing point – a new timber bridge that he had built along with the house. For now though, on this day, all was well.

The heat though was not relenting in the late afternoon sun. He could feel between his legs the warmth from the horse, sweating under the saddle. Of all of them, that horse deserved to reach the Rio Grande and drink deeply from its cooling waters and have the cold water wash away the dust from his hoofs. George realised his concentration was wandering, so he put those things out of his mind and concentrated on maintaining a steady trot.

Meanwhile, back at the house Joyce felt uneasy. Why was George late, had there been trouble? She looked at Fontaine's innocent face. Was this the best place to bring up a child? She had tried to make the house more presentable and homely for Christmas and had put a picture of Jesus on the living room table, lit by a single candle. She had considered a few paper chains but that seemed silly. They were so far from home, so far from a normal British Christmas. She stared out of the window and her persistence soon paid off; she noticed a little dust rising into the sultry air in the distance and, below it, a speck that moved. She quickly got out her opera glasses and looked, yes, it was them. She felt a sigh of relief.

"Rosina, I think they are coming. Can you heat up the samovar? Is everything ready for the men in the kitchen? George will be dying for a tea when he gets in. And is the library table clear, ready for him?"

"Yes, all is prepared."

"And is there enough food and drink and seats for the guards to sit and eat, and room for them to tie their mounts and water and feed them…"

"It is all arranged."

Joyce spent the next ten minutes checking and double checking that everything was well.

From the pampas George could now see his home, the building a brilliant white in colour, with its small green oasis of a garden at the front, all set beautifully against the blue-pink rock of the mountains beyond. He was beginning to feel more relaxed now. The lawless gauchos did not like to leave the pampas. That was their natural home where their horsemanship was unrivalled. They would no more leave the pampas than a fish would willingly leave the sea.

The next few minutes dragged for Joyce, as she waited expectantly. Finally she could hear the clip clop of the horses crossing the timber bridge over the river, and within a minute the horsemen had arrived at her door. George was very much in charge but it was Pedro, who spoke the best Spanish, who addressed the troop. Pedro was a tough-looking young man, with a handlebar moustache and big scar running across his face, perhaps a bit uncouth but clearly this had not dissuaded Rosina from marrying him and giving birth to their son Frederico.

"Unload the panniers and bring them into the house then you are free to go into the servants' quarters for food and drink. Make sure you tether the horses. And Carlos, you stay outside the house to keep guard and report any movements. Make sure Eduardo and Carlo do not leave the bridge."

George entered the house but had only had seconds to kiss Joyce and run his hand through Fontaine's curly hair, there was work to be done, and done quickly. The panniers, stuffed with the payroll money, were taken through to the library and he and Pedro closed the door, and sat down at the table, to allocate the funds into wage packets for the many workers at the ranch. The library door would remain shut while this went on. Rosina was in the kitchen with her mother making sure the troop was being looked after. They were a rough lot, and smelly and tired but cheerful now that food and drink were on tap.

Joyce looked out the window again. She should have felt secure. George knew what he was doing. A guard had been set by the front door and two other men were stationed on the timber bridge, which was the only feasible route from the pampas into the village.

Some time passed, the noise of the happy troopers in the kitchen was getting louder. She hoped that Rosina did not give them too much wine. Luckily there was another door out from the kitchen at the back so they would not have to pass through the house to get back to their mounts. She was not that happy with George for bringing so much money into the house either but she had to trust that he knew what he was doing. She glanced out of the window again. Then put down her knitting. The two men on the riverside, guarding the bridge, were nowhere to be seen. Suddenly the front door was pushed open, and to her shock, standing before her was a gang of men – four in all– armed to the teeth. She knew straight away that these were the outlaw gauchos by their long moustaches, red berets and knotted scarves. They hardly looked at her but instead headed straight for the library. She tried to scream but nothing came out. Almost at the same moment an almighty explosion went off in the kitchen, blowing the heavy timber door, which separated them from the morning room, off its hinges. Flames and smoke could be seen beyond, mingled with the screams of men. Instinctively she grabbed the bewildered Fontaine and pushed him behind the sofa. Black smoke was pouring out of the kitchen and she could hear the sound of men weeping and screaming in pain.

Concurrently with this were gunshots from the library. Then almost as soon as it had started, it ended – there was an eerie silence only broken by the wailing of injured men. Within a few seconds the four gauchos and Pedro were returning from the library with panniers over their shoulders. Where was George?

The answer came fast. She could see his body sprawled out on the library floor, through the open door. There was only one thing to be concluded from this: Pedro must have shot George. A total betrayal by his most trusted man. Pedro now stood in front of Joyce; he had a murderous look about him today that made your flesh creep. He smiled and reached out for his razor-sharp facon. In one movement he grabbed her with his hand holding her hair above the forehead and swung her around, so that she had her back to him, and then without pausing or giving any mercy, slashed her throat. The knife went in, barely making a sound and blood gushed out, so deep was the wound. She probably died immediately.

Fontaine stared from behind the sofa, he was shocked beyond words, unable to speak or shout or cry. The man smiled again, a cruel vicious sneer. Then within seconds they had gone. All of them.

He was alone. He crawled even further behind the sofa and waited, unable to move, almost unable to breathe. Finally he could hear a voice; it was Rosina's but very quiet. He looked around towards the kitchen and could see her crawling towards him. It looked as if half her face had been hurt so covered was it in blood. She saw Fontaine and plucked up the strength to reach out.

"Are you alright?" she whispered.

Finally he was able to answer through his dry mouth.

"Yes, but Ma is dead. They killed her."

She nodded gravely and surveyed the scene. She was clearly not well herself. The boy did not remember much more than this. Soon some villagers arrived. They were clearly shocked and made the sign of the cross over his mother. The boy was taken with Rosina to the villagers' homes where the old woman tried to comfort him, he could see in the next room them treating Rosina's wounds as best they could.

They were the only survivors: Rosina, Fontaine and the child Frederico. His mother, father, Maria and all the rest of the payroll troop were dead.

ONE

Ten Years Later.
October 1878, England

IT WAS NEVER EASY TO place what time of year it was, out here on the marshes. No trees to give you guidance with their tell-tale signs of reddening leaves, no flush of green in spring.

I knew that it was deep into October but the low sun beaming brightly on this forlorn place seemed intent on tricking you into believing it was still high summer.

We had come here, to this lonely single-track railway line, running parallel to the indented shoreline, because this was the scene of the horror. A death and the death of a young man, really just a boy. An old man, Edward Hope, stood ashen faced and firm as granite staring down the tracks, his eyes clear and steadfast in his gaze.

"This is it, Reeves; this is the place it happened. Fontaine's head severed from his body by a train. A cattle train running from Thames Haven towards London." He paused and collected his thoughts.

"Not a great end for a fourteen-year-old boy, is it?"

He looked distraught. I knew the boy was his grandson and that this death had hurt him to the core. There were questions to be asked but now it felt as if they would rub salt into the wounds, but I had to ask.

"Are the police still saying it's suicide?"

He grimaced.

"Of course, that is what it was made to look like. But I know who was responsible, and with your help I will see them hang for this."

The silence settled over us. I looked around. Nothing. Just marsh to the north, east and west with the Thames to the south. The only colour was the blood red sails of Thames barges moving upstream with the breeze. On the marshes themselves nothing moved apart from some grazing cattle in the distance.

There was something strange about a single railway line in the middle of nowhere. It ran dead straight for the most part, on a bed of gravel ballast, but to either side were no fences or trees or shrubs, or hedges. Perhaps it had been kept this way as it bounded the salting's, and on spring tides the seawater might lap over the rails, before ebbing back into the river.

I had been told the background in the carriage coming here: a processing station had been set up at Thames Haven where livestock had been imported from Argentina; from there they fatten them up, enough to make a better price. The trade was now ending due to changes in the law, making live imports more problematic, so it appeared the train line was little used.

I bent down and put my head against the iron rail. No

sound was forthcoming. Probably no trains today. Hope spoke slowly and in measured tones.

"Fontaine was staying with his aunt in Horndon for the holidays. They do not like the boarders staying at Harrow through the summer recess. He was a good lad, fine student by all accounts, and a good horseman. Taught him to ride while he was a nipper in the Argentine. I believe this was one of his rides, down from the village onto the marshes. I do not know why he came here. Matilda thinks he might have been sketching boats on the river or collecting seashells from the shore. We might never know for sure now. Maybe he just liked the solitude of this place."

"The problem with solitude," I responded…"is there are no witnesses. It might have been a terrible accident, or suicide, or foul play, how did the train driver react when it occurred?"

"He appears to have done all the right things. Stopped the train immediately, went back and inspected the body. He would have known straight away the lad was dead. Then reported it to the police and rail authorities. He said he did not see anything until he felt the bump. Who knows what the truth is, but I know Fontaine was a good and clever young man. He would not have played stupid pranks or taken his own life. I know that something bad happened here."

I kept my gaze.

"Go on."

"The man who owns these cattle-clearing stations at Thames Haven and most of the marshes is an Argentinean by the name of Romero, Alfonso Romero. I know that because I sold him this land a few years back. I thought we could have been partners, but we fell out badly. I can tell you that he is a nasty piece of work."

He paused.

"My grandson died here. On their land. By their train. It is too much of a coincidence. Something dark has happened here. That is why I want you to get to the bottom of it."

I looked back at him, then down onto the track.

"I'll do everything I can to get justice for Fontaine."

He nodded. Without a word we walked back to the pony and trap and with Hope taking the reins headed back towards Horndon.

It was just thirty minutes' ride away. The trap scuttled through the country lanes, past Stanford church and railway station then turned north at Pump Street before climbing up the hill to the village of Horndon.

We were greeted at High House, a fine detached two-storey house, by Hope's sister Matilda. Dressed all in black she tried to maintain a dignified air and soon had tea and biscuits ready for us. The house was large and well lived in. Matilda lived on her own most of the time and had probably enjoyed her time with young Fontaine for company. Now that was over, and you felt the darkness starting to take over again. She was probably a lonely old lady, set in her ways, but something in her eyes made you think she knew more than she said. Hope settled into a stout leather armchair and bade me to sit opposite him.

"I am going back to Buenos Aires tomorrow. So, I will be at sea for over a month and out of contact for at least six weeks. From then on telegrams can reach me at the ranch."

He reached for his pipe and started filling it.

"Any idea how we can get to the truth in all this?"

I looked around at the green patterned wallpaper, which looked like William Morris design. I was struggling to find anything positive to say.

"Not easily, I fear. My strategy will be dig and dig, then dig some more. I will try to find out what skeletons that Romero is hiding. Something he wanted to keep secret that perhaps, maybe, Fontaine stumbled across."

Hope gave a thin smile.

"My thoughts exactly. I think you could begin with the registered office of Thames Haven Limited. It is in Thames Street, right by Fenchurch Street station. See if you can interview Romero."

I nodded.

"That is a starting point at least."

He continued.

"I also have some good contacts in the city. Chap named Bill Barrington. Works in shipping. He will probably know Romero, by reputation at least, he knows everyone. So, if there is any gossip, he will have it. Here are his details."

Hope opened a small notebook, which he kept in his tweed jacket pocket. Wrote down some details, tore out the page, and handed it over.

"He is a bit of a character. Likes a drink. Romero is a drinker as well. Says it is to kill the pain of his old injuries. Not sure if that's true. Then truth be told I am not sure anything Romero says is the truth."

I decided to press him a little more.

"Tell me about the background to your dislike of each other."

Hope wriggled in his chair making himself more comfortable.

"As you know I was in the Engineers, back before the war in Crimea. Thought I was going to be in the army all my life. Then an opportunity came up to be a surveyor, and of all places halfway across the world in Argentina. They were just looking at possible routes for railways, so I went to survey the land. Anyway, I soon realised that the country was a gold mine for cattle farmers. Now my son George had established himself in the livestock business around this part of Essex. I persuaded him to come to the Argentine and give it a go, so he moved out there with his new wife Joyce and their baby Fontaine. A brave decision. To cut a long story short, it went very well indeed. You see there are thousands of square miles of grassland out there, perfect for livestock grazing, and you can buy the land for a song. In fact a lot of people don't even do that, they just fence off land and say it is theirs, which is the sort of place it is… At the same time shipping routes were opening between the Argentine and Britain. Everyone in the livestock game could make their fortunes. That is where I met Romero – he was from gaucho stock but had been educated along the way, he couldn't ride very well anymore because of his injuries. We started out as friends, but it did not last. The old deadly sin: greed, avarice, that's what got into Romero and ruined everything. Trouble is there are too many opportunities out there to make a fortune by breaking the rules. The country is too much like the Wild West. Precious little law and order, there is a lot of cattle rustling and land grabbing, not an easy place to do business. Nothing to protect the law-abiding rancher."

He paused for breath.

"I had set up George and Joyce in a brand new home, a hacienda in Sierra de la Ventana, about thirty miles north-east of Bahia Blanca in the lea of the mountains at the southern edge of the pampas. The mountains are a wonderful sight, particularly when the grey blue and pink rocks on the faces are glowing in the sunshine. The village has its own river, the Rio Sauce Grande, and all around the house were Espinal woodlands with Acacias and Ceibo trees with their scarlet blooms in spring.

"It was like a little piece of England, transported to South America but still within close range of the cattle stations on the pampas.

"They settled in and all seemed well. Then George did something a bit silly, in retrospect, he, along with his chief clerk Pedro Diaz and an armed guard, brought home the payroll from the bank. It was late afternoon and in the coolest room of the house, the library, they set about dividing it up and packaging it, to be taken to the cattle station. However it appears that Pedro was not to be trusted, despite being almost part of the family, he was even married to Rosina, Fontaine's nanny, and had his own child, Frederico who lived in the house. Anyway there was a shot in the library and George was dead, then the front door was smashed down and gauchos appeared brandishing pistols. Joyce had witnessed all this and knew Pedro must be the killer, so he killed her in cold blood as well. Cut the poor girl's throat. The soldiers, who were supposed to be guarding them, were in the servants' kitchen eating and drinking. The bandits threw a bomb into the middle of the room, pretty much killed them all. Only the nanny and her child survived. She was helping out serving them and got caught in the blast as well and was badly injured but lived."

He was clearly upset.

"It was vicious, ruthless. My whole family all dead within minutes. The bandits took all the money and even some jewellery which belonged to Joyce.

"Nearby villagers came to see what had occurred but by then the bandits had crossed the Rio Sauce Grande and were heading north-east at speed across the pampas.

"I was away in Buenos Aires at the time, oddly enough with Romero, concluding a business deal. I raced back as soon as I heard. Luckily, Fontaine had survived the massacre somehow; they think he hid behind the sofa, but he was traumatised by what had happened. The local police did their best but we had no clue as to who the bandits were. The only lead we got was a month or so later where some of the jewellery turned up at a market in Bahia Blanca. I did all I could. Luckily Fontaine had caught sight of the man who killed his mother, I say luckily – it must have broken the lad's heart. Anyway he managed to give us a description of the killer and I had a picture of him, a likeness, produced and put up all over the country along with a massive reward for any information leading to his arrest. Sad to say the killer was one of George's own men Pedro, so he was totally betrayed. Finally Pedro was found, arrested and taken to prison awaiting trial. Then somehow he escaped from that gaol. My guess is that somehow the prison guards were bribed to turn the other cheek. Then nothing since. He just disappeared. That was almost ten years ago and some of the posters are still up to this day."

He was still clearly distraught.

"And that was that. Life has to carry on. I redecorated their house and moved in myself, making sure I stepped up security of course. I've now got a wall around the property with only one main gate, which is always closed. At the time of the killings Fontaine was only four, coming on five, and was now an orphan. Problem was that I live on my own with just a housekeeper. My dear wife Dorothy had died many years ago. So, looking after a young lad was difficult for me. Anyway, I took him under my wings but decided that he should have an English education. So sent him to England and eventually got him into Harrow, where he was a boarder, and was doing well there until this."

He paused to gather his thoughts.

"Time has passed but I am still angry about those murders, and I would dearly love to bring whoever did it to justice. And now after all my attempts to keep him safe, Fontaine is dead… It is almost too much to bear."

I probed a bit further.

"So what is your relationship to Romero?"

"I am afraid I backed the wrong horse with him. He was from gaucho stock originally but had lost the use of much of the left side of his body due to a vicious knife wound in the neck cutting his nerves. Don't know what the fight was about. He never mentioned it. Anyway I gave him a job helping me with the ledgers at the ranch. He did well so he almost became a sort of partner. Being a local, his Spanish was stronger than mine, so he was a good communicator. At the time I was pushing the idea of exporting cattle to England. We were taking the cattle in boats to the Thames estuary then putting them to pasture on the marshlands and fattening them up for going to market in London. After a while it was obvious that it was too big of an operation to run myself from my base in the Argentine so I sent Romero over to England to set up a London office and oversee the operation. It went well for a while. But communication over such a distance was hard. So, after three years or so I let him buy me out. I sold him all the land on the Stanford marshes and gave him complete control. Stupidly I forgot to cover my back. I should have read the small print in our contract, but I've never been a man for detail, I always prefer a handshake to a written agreement, more fool me... Before I knew it, he was using other cattle merchants and even his own boat. I was effectively cut out of the very operation I had started. That was the reason for the fallout. Worse still I now think he might have had something to do with the attack on George and Joyce. I cannot prove it as Pedro and his gaucho friends did all the killing but the thought is still there in the back of my mind."

Matilda arrived with the tea. For the next hour I sat around talking with Matilda and Edward. Both had very warm memories of Fontaine, and at times they were both close to tears. Matilda even broke off and returned with one of the lad's sketchbooks and handed it to Edward who then passed it on to me. The book was full of sketches of boats, mostly Thames barges but steamers as well. Mostly in black and white, but Fontaine had clearly got a liking for the red ochre of the barges' sails and used this colour as well. Even the barges with red paintwork had this carefully coloured in along with their red flags.

I finally handed the book back to Edward.

"Well at least we know one of the reasons he visited the marshes. He had an eye for the boats and drawing from what I can see."

"Indeed, but I have looked at these many times and can find nothing substantial to indicate that he had trodden on

Romero's toes. They are, what they seem, sketches from a boy with a good eye and steady hand."

Finally, the afternoon reached its end. Dusk was falling. Hope kindly took me down in his trap to Stanford station where we shook hands. I looked him in the eye.

"I will do my absolute best; of that you can be sure."

He nodded.

"I know you will."

At that we bade farewell, and I caught the train back into London.

TWO

The City

NEXT DAY I ARRIVED AT the offices of Thames Haven Limited, a couple of minutes' walk from Fenchurch Street. The city of London was bustling, as always. The streets were thronged with hansom cabs and gentlemen in dark suits and bowler hats going about their business. Poorly dressed children ran behind the cabs scooping up the horse dung and putting it into buckets. Even by this small act you could see London was a town of the 'haves' and 'have nots'.

The offices were in a fine modern building with large timber doors leading via an oak-panelled corridor to a reception desk. Behind this was a middle-aged man with a bald head and spectacles, perched below his eye line for reading. He looked up. I introduced myself and proffered an outstretched hand.

"Good morning, I am William Reeves, shipping agent. I wonder if it would be possible to talk to the director of Thames Haven Limited, who I believe is Mr Alfonso Romero..."

The man looked me up and down.

"What business do you have?" He did not waste his words.

"I am enquiring on behalf of a Mr Edward Hope. His particular interest is the railway line linking your works at Thames Haven to the main Tilbury to Southend line and an unfortunate incident that occurred this summer. Namely the death of his grandson Fontaine Hope."

The man stared impassively.

"Mr Romero is not available for meetings. I also believe that the incident you refer to was fully investigated and the coroner stated it was a death by misadventure. So sadly, we must assume that the matter is now closed."

I stood rooted to the ground, stunned by his cold, business-like response. He continued.

"For your information, I am Edgar Wise, the chief clerk for Thames Haven Limited, and therefore a man of some authority, so you can report that back to Mister Hope if you so wish."

I looked beyond the man and over the screen behind him and could see a female clerk surreptitiously looking, and perhaps listening, to our conversation. She was probably in her late thirties with dark hair in a tight bob. Beyond her I could see no other staff; I had to assume Romero had his private office somewhere well out of sight.

I decided there was nothing to be had here.

"Well thank you, Mister Wise, for your candour. I will bid you good day."

At that I turned and walked out back into the street, aware that Wise's eyes followed me all the way.

It was now mid-morning. What to do next? I decided

to spend the next two hours in the public reading area of Lloyds checking out shipping movements. It was tedious work, but a picture was starting to emerge of the business interests of Thames Haven and the number of their shipping movements. It was clear that this company were major players in Anglo-Argentina trade. Even though cargoes of cattle had almost ceased there was still a healthy trade in salted beef and a new cannery in Fray Bentos, on the east coast of the Argentine, was beginning to export their wares… Thames Haven, it seemed, was still the port of choice for these imported goods.

It was now almost lunchtime and two hours staring at ledgers was more than enough. On a hunch I decided to return to Fenchurch Street and find some suitable tearooms for refreshment. I soon found one within sight of Romero's offices on the junction of Thames Street, it was a nice-looking café clearly aimed at the lunchtime city trade. On entering the tearoom my eyes were drawn to the far corner, where, sitting alone, was the female clerk I had noticed standing in Romero's offices. Luckily, she had not noticed me, so I sat down at the next table along to hers.

She was engrossed in reading a newspaper and did not notice me until I ordered some tea and toast from the waitress. She glanced up on hearing my voice then quickly hid back behind her paper.

This lady intrigued me. She had the white blouse and dark jacket you would expect but her face had a pronounced but attractive nose, below deep brown eyes. Her hair, which was parted in the centre, was tied up in a tight bob but with a fine fringe falling down over her forehead, almost down to her eyebrows. I noticed she had some scarring on her right cheek which then ran up into her forehead, perhaps that is why she styled her hair that way. The scarring was not that worrying though, just some areas of rougher pink skin, perhaps she had been in a fire at some point.

She appeared very self-contained and comfortable in this tearoom. She obviously liked her own company and presumably came here to get away from the office.

This was too good a chance to miss. I asked politely, "Have you got any sugar on your table, I am afraid the waitress seems to have forgotten mine?"

She looked up from her paper. There was an odd beauty about her.

"Of course. There you are."

She delicately picked up the sugar pot and handed it to me. Front on I noticed her scarring was worse than I first thought, but she seemed confident enough in her demeanour.

I smiled.

"Excuse me for being forward but I could not help noticing that you work in Thames Haven's offices. I was there only this morning."

She was not happy at this. The awkwardness filled the air. She responded quietly, "I think you must be mistaken, sir. I work in the back office and did not see you."

I smiled again.

"I understand. No doubt it is a relief to get away from the office and come to this fine tearoom?"

She seemed to find this comment even more distasteful.

"I must ask you, sir, not to be so forward. I am only here to have lunch and read my newspaper; which I prefer to do in silence."

I knew this conversation had ended.

"I apologise for interrupting your lunch hour, it was discourteous of me. Please do not let it spoil your meal."

At that we both resumed our solitary dining. I noticed that she was reading assiduously, gently turning over the pages and treating the paper with the utmost respect. Finally she finished the reading, tucked the paper under her arm and then left, and, I assume, returned to the offices, making sure to thank the owner of the tearoom on the way out.

Somehow, I knew that she was important to this case. Beyond that she had an unusual attractiveness, which I found interesting and mysterious.

THREE

Big Bill

THE NEXT DAY I RETURNED to the city. Today I was meeting Bill Barrington, a friend of Hope's and a man, I was told, with a vast knowledge of the city and shipping, and hopefully Romero. It was just coming up to one thirty as I left Fenchurch Street station, so I decided to casually walk past the tearooms I had frequented yesterday. Just as I did so the girl from Romero's office emerged, on her own, going back to the office. So, I thought, this was her routine: same café, same time, probably the same seat, every working day. Always useful to know. I turned and walked back past the oddly named 'French Ordinary Court' to the 'Cheshire Cheese' public house, located directly under the railway bridge.

It was very busy, but I ordered a pint of bitter and waited for Bill Barrington to arrive. I did not have to wait long. A giant of a man entered the inn, with a red nose below watchful eyes that missed nothing. He had a fine beer gut that crept over the top of his trousers. He was probably in his forties. On the top of his head perched a bowler hat which seemed almost too small for such a large man. He clearly knew everyone. After some cursory greetings to the publican, and some other people in the bar, he came over to me and outstretched his hand.

"Bill Barrington. Good to meet you."

"William Reeves."

In no time we were talking. About everything. Clearly this public house was Bill's domain – though you got the feeling that every hostelry would be his kingdom. I brought up the subject of Romero and what did Bill know of him. The big man seemed to talk slowly and more quietly than before.

"I know Romero fairly well. He came over from the Argentine a few years back. Had some bits of business with him but nothing to write home about. His company are pretty big now though. Fingers in a lot of pies. That is about all I know of his business. On a personal level, he is a big drinker and a womaniser. Got a noticeable limp but that doesn't seem to put the fillies off. You will see that when he arrives. Best if we keep our distance though."

I took all this in.

"What about his office. How does that run?"

"He has an old codger, Edgar Wise, who does most of the work, also a clerk, Elisa Pound I think her name is, who is in the back office. I think she must do contracts in English and Spanish because he is still a bit wobbly with his English speaking."

"What does she look like?"

He smiled.

"Fairly fit. Late thirties, dark hair, dark eyes. Got some scarring on her cheek? Don't know the story behind that.

Don't think she is a type though, if you have interests in that direction."

I felt caught out by this.

"Type. What do you mean?"

Barrington never got to answer as through the doors came a man whose appearance immediately set him apart from the crowd. Tall and sturdy looking with a big mouth and dark eyebrows and above that a mop of black curly hair. He had a prize fighter's neck which made it look as if his shoulders were touching the sides of his ears. I guessed him to be in his late thirties or early forties. His face was one big smile, although his skin looked greasy, and his dark brown eyes had a cruel glint to them. Not a man to be trusted, a man who had seen the world.

I knew this was my man. Bill gave a wry smile.

"You watch. Straight over to the barmaid."

He was spot on.

I looked at Bill, not sure if he would greet Romero. Bill made no move.

"Probably best if we keep a low profile. As I say I have had no dealings with him for some time, so he probably does not remember me. You might learn more by just observing him and how he works the room."

We chatted for a few more minutes. Romero was clearly everyone's friend and his conversations, which were out of earshot, were often punctuated by new people coming into the pub and shaking his hand and offering greetings. I glanced at my companion, he was obviously getting bored.

"This place is all about business. Let us try out some other bars."

At that we left.

A few minutes' walk and we entered another hostelry. Again, Bill drank happily, and a lot. Clearly his lunchtime drinking was on an enormous scale, something I had not done for years. I had an awful feeling that this was just a normal day at the office for him. Our conversation drifted from the professional to personal seamlessly. Bill thought that Romero had got his fingers burnt by ploughing so much money into the jetty at Thames Haven.

"He got well stitched up there. No sooner were they importing Argentine cattle into the country than the local farmers got up in arms. Claimed that the South American cattle were introducing diseases into the livestock population, ruining their businesses. All bollocks of course, but the government bought it and stopped live animal imports. Now he is using his railhead for importing salted beef. Good luck there. He would be better bringing it into the pool of London and closing that place down."

I just nodded, this was not my field of expertise but I was sure Bill knew his stuff.

Time marched on. Some of the lunchtime trade thinned. We carried on to another pub, closer to the river. Again, the conversation and the beer flowed. Finally, he set off to the latrines to relieve himself. I pulled my fob watch out of my top pocket. Almost three o'clock. The pubs would close soon, and I could give my liver a rest.

He came back beaming.

"Almost three. We had better get down to the Lovat Arms. Just up from the market."

I must have looked perplexed.

"It is coming up to three o'clock, Bill. The pub will be shut soon."

He laughed.

"Not the Lovat. They have a special licence – for the fish porters down at Billingsgate. The market has been open from before dawn and closes at three, so it is for them to get a beer in after work."

We then marched off down the narrow streets towards the river. I say marched. For me it was becoming more of a stumble. I was just not used to this level of drinking.

We entered the Lovat, and I could immediately smell the fish from the market men.

Bill sensed my discomfort.

"Don't worry, you will soon get used to the fishy smell. Throw another lump of coal on the fire, that should take the edge off it."

He pointed to a mean fire in a dirty grate, which seemed to be exuding more than its fair share of smoke. The kindest thing I can think to say about the pub was that it looked a little tired. The floor was covered in thick sawdust and the exhausted market porters were mostly slumped in the available seating, smoking tobacco from their short clay pipes. I turned to Bill.

"Lovat Arms, good name, I wonder if it was named after the old Jacobite, Lord Lovat, who got executed down the road at Tower Green?"

Bill nodded. "Probably, can't say I've ever thought about it."

I continued.

"Of course, the public execution by sword was in the last century; which to be honest is probably about the last time they had their chimneys cleaned in here, by the smell of that fire."

Bill smiled. "It helps to mask the fishy smell."

At this he got the drinks in. I noticed he was on first name terms with the barmaid. A mousy blonde who looked as if she never washed her hair, poor skin as well, under cheap makeup, she had the kind of friendly but tired look that gave the impression you might get more than beer at this inn.

No sooner had we started drinking than in walked Romero. It was his typical Latin entrance, despite the pronounced limp, which seemed to invite the other regulars to look at him and admire his presence in their lowly inn. He had a constant smile which showed off his thick lips and teeth. But his dark brown eyes were less friendly, watchful and were soon preoccupied by the barmaid. He was soon all over her. To me he appeared to be a man with no class at all but the sort of easy swagger that attracts some women. I looked at Bill, who guessed my question.

"That is one of his wenches. Nettie Kelly. Bit of a type. Comes from a family of them. Her sister has a pub down at North Woolwich and she is just as bad. I've seen Nettie take the regulars round the back for a bit of 'how's your father'. That's how brazen she is."

I pointed out something that I had noticed earlier.

"Her name was above the door as being a licensed victualler, along with a Mr Kelly."

Bill shrugged.

"He spends most of his time in the backroom. He is a heavy drinker, an alcoholic, can hardly walk up the stairs. Gets so drunk he pisses himself. She runs this pub and makes sure the tills keep ringing."

We carried on drinking. I sensed it was best that Romero

did not know of our presence, so we kept a safe distance. We were here to watch and observe, not confront the man.

After some time had elapsed, no idea how long as I had stopped looking at my fob watch. Another man arrived and immediately went over to Romero.

He was a very British looking man with a military bearing and fine moustache, slightly greying – a bit older than Romero. The moustache did not quite cover a port-wine stain he had on his cheek. Strangely, that reminded me of someone.

The two men talked away. Clearly Romero's English was good enough. I could not hear their conversation but despite their obviously shared interest in the barmaid, it was clearly about a business matter. The day wore on. Finally, we both seemed to decide enough was enough.

"I'd better look into the office, see how things are going," said Bill.

I concurred that I had much to do. We left together, me walking, almost stumbling, back to Fenchurch Street and him taking another turning. It had been a long lunchtime.

FOUR

Woolwich

I HAD AN UNSETTLED NIGHT's sleep after my lunchtime session with Bill. Something was playing on my mind; it was the identity of the man in the pub with the port-wine stain. I knew him from somewhere. Finally, it came to me. He was in the Engineers. We had trained together at the military academy in Woolwich, and then gone over to Crimea. By the look of him he might still be in the military as he had that upright, almost awkward, posture that comes from years of drill.

For some reason I felt he was important to understanding Romero's business, so I hatched a plan.

Two days later I arrived at the door of Woolwich Academy, the home of the Royal Engineers and Royal Artillery companies. It was an easy trip, a train to North Woolwich, then ferry to the south bank, then ten minutes' walk. I had decked myself out in the remains of my old uniform and was soon in discussion with the porter, a young man, at the main entrance.

"Good morning. Let me introduce myself, I am William Reeves, Royal Engineer, retired. I am trying to organise a get together for all the Engineers who served with me at Crimea."

The porter looked perplexed.

"You see the war started in early 1854 and so now we are in October 1878, it will soon be the twenty-fifth anniversary."

The porter seemed to grasp this.

"So, you want to meet up with your old colleagues."

"Indeed. That is the idea."

"I will call on Sergeant Major Hammond. He was here in the fifties so he might be able to help you."

I was much relieved. I remembered him from my training days.

"Is that Howard Hammond. Is he still here?"

"Indeed he is. If you could wait here."

Five minutes later a balding man, probably now almost sixty years of age, appeared. I just about recognised him. I smiled and proffered my hand.

"Sergeant Major Hammond. I do not know if you remember me: William Reeves. I trained here in 1852?"

He looked at me for a moment, and then smiled.

"Reeves? Yes, of course. You went off to Crimea. I take it you are not in the military now. What can I do for you?"

I then went through my story of hoping to arrange a get together of the veterans and mentioned that I was particularly interested in finding Henry Frankland. The answer came back straight away; he was still in the military and was located just a mile down the road at Woolwich Arsenal. Even better he worked there in a 'nine to five' job.

To keep my cover story going I then spent quite a while going through names and finding out their whereabouts. Most had left the military, but I was not that interested, it was Frankland that I had come for.

After an hour of friendly reminiscing, I bade farewell.

The next day I returned to Woolwich, late in the afternoon, but it was to the arsenal this time. I stood outside the main gates, just out of sight, and waited for the five o'clock bell. My wait was not in vain. Within minutes Frankland emerged amongst a throng of workers. I waited then followed him. It was soon obvious he was heading towards the nearby ferry stage, so he must now live north of the river. I kept my distance, but followed him down onto the jetty and awaited the ferry. It manoeuvred into position and the gangplank came down. Frankland was one of the first on; I followed at a discreet distance. Within minutes we were in mid-river. I could see him, but he did not see me. Then it was the disembarkation. Again, he was off quickly. I expected him to walk straight into North Woolwich station, only yards away, but instead he carried on down the road and disappeared into the Royal Standard pub, located alongside the North Woolwich pleasure gardens. It should be mentioned here that the gardens had a reputation for mollies – women of the street. The pleasure gardens were now going out of fashion, but the mollies remained, and did steady business. Luckily, it was now well past five and getting dark, so the gates were shut. I could not help noticing though an unusually large number of ladies standing around near the entrance at discreet distances from each other. Clearly playtime went on beyond the park's opening hours.

I walked into the pub and could immediately see Henry

leaning on the bar talking to the barmaid. I looked at the sign above the entrance door: Stanley Hobbs and Mary Kelly Licensed Victuallers. So, it looked as if the lady behind the bar was indeed the sister of Nettie Kelly.

For a while I kept myself to myself and drank a pint of bitter away from them. I had soon seen enough. Clearly, they were in some kind of relationship. He was obsessed with her, constantly reaching out and holding her hands. She was laughing at everything he said. Time for me to intervene.

"Henry. Isn't it?"

He looked at me bemused and somewhat annoyed at the interruption.

"Henry Frankland. You remember me. William Reeves, Royal Engineers, we trained together at Woolwich back in the fifties."

He looked at me more closely.

"Of course Reeves. What are you doing here?"

I smiled.

"I will not disturb you too long. Just wanted to tell you that I am organising a twenty-fifth anniversary get together of the Engineers who went to Crimea. Wondered if you would be interested?"

He looked me up and down.

"Might well be, old boy. I am a bit busy at the moment. If I give you my address, you can send me details when it is all organised."

He then pulled a small notepad out of his pocket and began writing. I filled in the silence.

"What are you doing with yourself these days?"

"I am still with the military, based at the arsenal now. Here you are."

He handed me the scrap of paper with his address. There was a slight silence that I hoped he would fill, he did.

"So, what are you getting up to these days, Reeves?"

"I am into shipping. Spend most of my time in the city – still looking to find the perfect job though."

Mary made her excuses and went off to serve other customers. I continued.

"I had a good offer only last month. Chap called Romero, wanted me to drop everything and go out to the Argentine surveying."

I could see Henry's face whitening at this.

"Of course, I turned him down, too old to make that kind of change now. Have you ever come across Romero? Alfonso Romero runs some kind of operation called Thames Haven Limited."

Henry stumbled over his words.

"Cannot say I have ever come across him. Now, if you can excuse me, I have got some business to do with the landlady. Nice meeting you after all this time."

He stuck out his hand. I shook it. I could not help noticing it was cold and sweaty.

"Hope to see you at the reunion then."

He replied, "By the way, how did you know to find me here?"

"I just asked some of the old boys at Woolwich. They said you were always in the Royal Standard at this time of day."

He was not smiling at this.

I quickly finished my pint, said farewell, and left the pub. I had all that I came for.

FIVE

Train to the Thames

I WENT HOME AND ARRANGED another meeting with Bill. Within a few days we were back at the Cheshire Cheese, and he had some information for me.

"You are in luck. I have found out that a ship is leaving Thames Haven next week bound for the Argentine."

I smiled gleefully; this was what I needed.

"Any clue about the cargo?"

"Looks like mostly farm machinery going out and corned beef coming in. It will be on the twenty-ninth October, so assuming they follow the tides it will probably depart about four in the afternoon. In fact, Thames Haven have put out the word for dockers who want a day's work. They will be taken down in the train with the goods for export. Presumably, they will help unload the corn beef and load the machinery on board the boat. It will take a few hours, depending on how many men they have, and how organised they are. My guess is half the hired labour will be Irish who are a bit hit and miss. The dockers in regular employment would not be interested."

This was the break I had been waiting for.

"Any chance of me getting on the train to observe what goes on?"

"Should not be a problem. I've a friend who works on the freight trains going out of Fenchurch Street. I will organise it for you."

"That would be great. Many thanks."

"All you need to do is get yourself to Fenchurch Street at eight o'clock in the morning. I will arrange for you to get slipped onto the train. Find yourself somewhere comfortable, as it will be a long day. My guess is that the front carriages will have the goods for export and behind them a passenger carriage for the dockers. There will also be a couple of Customs and Excise officers on board who will oversee things at the Thames Haven end. Does that all sound good to you?"

"Could not be better."

We had a good drink to celebrate then I made my excuses and left. This was a golden opportunity to see what was going on at the Thames Haven jetty.

On the twenty-ninth October I arrived at Fenchurch Street well before the allotted time and quickly found the guard, a friend of Bill's, who secreted me at the back of the guard's van. The train was made up of mostly freight carriages with only one carriage put aside for passengers. These soon arrived. Much as Bill had told me, they were mostly Irish, a dozen or so of them. At nine precisely the train moved off and we set off towards our destination. I kept conversation with the guard, whose name was Alf, down to a minimum in case any of the dockers overheard me. Within ten minutes we had stopped at Limehouse, on the new station which crossed the Highway at height. There were more dockers here and I kept my head down in case they inadvertently entered the guard's van. I could hear a particularly bellicose foreman ushering them onto the train. By the sound of his instructions I fully expected him to get a cane out and beat any latecomers. Within a minute we were off. The train was now leaving the London docklands and the sprawl of back-to-back houses and going out onto the empty marshlands. Stations came and went: Barking, Rainham, Purfleet. The train did not stop again until Tilbury Fort, where we took on two official-looking gentlemen. I guessed they must be the Customs and Excise men. The train travelled on in an easterly direction and just past Low Street Halt we turned right onto the single-track branch line that I had visited with Hope. Here there was nothing but marsh and grazing animals, mostly cattle. The river to my right and the enormous sky above. Ten minutes later we were stopping at Thames Haven itself.

What can be said of this place? Clearly it was not in regular use anymore. The whole site had a forlorn look about it. The only building was a single sizeable black timber cattle shed, which was to the east of the existing platform, and this had weeds growing up around it. Beyond the buffers, south there was a ship moored there now, an iron steamship with twin funnels.

The train pulled up very slowly, with its engine now close to the buffers. From here it was facing directly on to the port bow of the steamship, sitting alongside the jetty. Clearly any loading would have to be done without the aid of cranes or even cargo nets; both the import and export goods would have to be manhandled from ship to the train. It appeared a ramp had been put into place for this purpose, linking the land on the foreshore with the ship. I wondered how this was going to work. The tidal range on this part of the Thames was about twenty feet and with twelve hours between high tides they would have to work quickly. Clearly this set-up was designed for herding cattle off boats, not crated goods.

These deficiencies seemed not to worry the dockers and foreman who were already wheeling crates from the freight wagons along the timber ramp onto the ship's deck. At the same time goods were being taken out of the ship's hold and wheeled on cargo trolleys and the like over the ramp onto the train platform. They would have to get a move on before the tide dropped, and they did! There was a flurry of activity – crates being dragged off the boat, a constant noise of shouting and orders, mostly from the bellicose foreman, and the clanking of goods being loaded and unloaded. I only had a limited view of this work as I was peeking through the guard's van window. One thing was clear, this cattle dock was not ideal for what they were doing. I can only assume that Romero, having invested so much in building it, was determined to get value for money.

Tired of my restricted view, I bade goodbye to the guard Alf, slipping him a sovereign for his trouble and creeping out onto the jetty. Luckily as I was at the back of the train, and all the frenetic activity was near the front, it was easy to slip away. Hopefully, if I was seen, they might mistake me for the guard leaving the train for a leak. The storage shed was only about a couple of chains distant, so I stealthily covered the ground and slipped behind it. From this vantage point, I could see the loading operation in full swing. I could also see more of the steamship, its name was *River Plate* and it had clearly seen many years of service. The twin funnels occasionally belched out dirty smoke despite it standing at rest. The bravery of the seamen who travelled halfway around the world in all weathers on boats like this never ceased to amaze me.

I had been hoping to see something untoward, but nothing was in any way suspicious. The dockers worked away incessantly and without any breaks for almost two hours. The Excise officers oversaw everything that was occurring. The foreman never stopped shouting and the seamen on the *River Plate* also worked hard to unload their cargo and to take on the goods.

After a while I could see that the tide was turning and the river dropping. The timber ramps, which had originally climbed from the jetty to the boat, now went down onto it. Finally, it was all done.

The last of the crates were hauled onto the boat, and the Excise officers spoke to the foreman. The boat's captain, I assume from his uniform, also came on shore briefly to speak to them. There were handshakes all round and after this the captain departed and the ramps were pushed back onto the jetty. The ship then fired its boilers up and even more dark smoke came out of the funnels, filling the air with its acrid smell. I was surprised that this boat could even make the journey all the way to the Argentine as it looked as if it had seen better days. A seaman threw the hawsers onto the jetty and slowly the ship left the pier and manoeuvred towards the deeper waters of the estuary.

The dockers lined up at a fold-up table and were paid. Despite their tiredness and ragged appearance, they behaved well; clearly, they were getting paid what had been agreed without argument.

The Excise officers and foreman rejoined the train. The hired hands, now with money in their pockets, dragged their tired bodies back into the passenger carriage and within minutes the train had departed with the engine pushing the carriages up the track, back towards Fenchurch Street.

There was one man left on the platform, a swarthy looking gent with a dark black rain coat, suitable for riding and walking in all weathers. Immediately after the train departed he wandered off to check the shed and surrounding land, I assumed he was some kind of night watchman. I kept my head down; I did not want to be found out so late in the day. I could hear the man checking doors and locks, making sure the empty sheds were secure. He finished off his chores by looking along the platform, presumably in the hope of finding some dropped coins from the tired dockers, but from what I could see, he found nothing. It was now raining and the marshland mist was settling onto the scene.

Content that all was safely secured, the man walked over to a sturdy looking horse that had waited patiently all day, and after unfastening it from its tether, mounted it and rode off. I kept my eyes on his movements for a while. He was heading due north, presumably to Fobbing village, which, as the crow flies, was the nearest settlement to Thames Haven. After he had disappeared into the rainy mist, I breathed a sigh of relief.

I was now all alone in the middle of nowhere. It was little past midday. I had decided to make way by foot to Fobbing, less than three miles' distance, but as the night watchman was also going in that direction, I decided instead to simply retrace my steps back along the track the four miles to Stanford village. Unfortunately, on these marshy saltings it would not be possible to take any short cuts without the risk of sinking into hidden ditches full of saltwater. I sat disconsolate and took out my precious chocolate bar. The only food I had brought with me.

While eating that I cast my eye towards the *River Plate*, she was going slowly, far more cautious than I would have ever thought. The train was now long gone. Just as I was about to make tracks back towards Stanford, I noticed something odd. The ship changed course and headed back towards the coast but perhaps half a mile further downriver. At about this point was an old ship, moored close to the marshy shoreline, I could just see from its red triangular warning sign and red flag and markings that it was probably a gunpowder boat, which is a stationary boat moored in an isolated area and used to store munitions. It would be just outside the port of London area and far enough away from habitation to create no damage if an explosion occurred. Oddly, unless I was mistaken the *River Plate* was heading straight for it. I took my opera glasses from my jacket pocket and looked closely. I could now see men on the deck of the gunpowder boat waving to the Argentine ship. Something was wrong here.

I decided to take a closer look. There was no seawall as such along this part of the coastline but clearly at some time in the past a rudimentary earth bank, a simple embankment, had been created to hold back the river. Inland from this, a few feet distant, was a ditch. By walking with a pronounced stoop within the ditch, I was able to get closer to the boats without being visible. I moved very slowly, knowing that it would be movement that would catch the eye of any seamen on lookout. Luckily, there was a lot of overgrown sedge and grasses to shield my passage. At about a furlong from the boats the ditch ran out, so I lay down and viewed the scene with my glasses. What I saw came as a complete surprise. On the deck of the gunpowder boat were three men calling out to the seamen on the *River Plate* and one of these men, and clearly the person in charge, was Henry Frankland himself!

I also noticed that tucked behind the gunpowder boat was a sailing barge which looked as if it had 'Woolwich Arsenal' insignia written on its side. So, what was going on? My answer came in seconds, boxes were being loaded into the cargo nets and manoeuvred over to the deck of the *River Plate*. It can only be one thing, boxes of dynamite, and there was no way this could be a legitimate transaction. I got the picture now. Surplus, out of date explosives, and perhaps ammunition as well, were taken by barge from the arsenal along the river to the gunpowder boat, under Frankland's direction no doubt. Then these explosives were sold to the Argentineans and slipped into the hold of their boat far away from the prying eyes of the Customs and Excise officers. Perhaps this is why young Fontaine was killed. Perhaps the innocent sketches of a boat showing the red flag of a gunpowder boat had spooked those on board the boat? Did he stumble across this activity and feel the wrath of these crooks? I was letting my imagination run away with me.

I lay on the wet ground and watched for some time, aware that any movement could catch the sailors' eyes. In half an hour it was all over. A substantial number of boxes and crates had been transferred from the gunpowder boat into the hold of the *River Plate*. A bag, perhaps carrying money, was thrown from the Argentine boat and caught by Frankland. He opened the bag and counted the contents, then clearly content, gave a thumbs-up sign. The Argentine boat slowly moved out from the inshore waters, away from the gunpowder boat, and out towards the centre of the Thames estuary. The transfer was over.

Meanwhile Frankland was not hanging about, he and another member of the crew climbed down the rope ladder into the sailing barge which was moored alongside, and were soon setting up the sails. The ropes were released and in no time the boat was drifting serenely on the Thames with its bow facing upriver towards London. I noted a crew of two were left on board the gunpowder boat; perhaps it was their job to guard it at all times. What a joke. This was clearly a fiddle of the highest order and Frankland was at the centre of it. Presumably, the barge was going back to Woolwich arsenal where he would organise the paperwork to look like only surplus explosives had been taken to the moored boat for safe storage, perhaps prior to disposal. Only in this case the 'disposal' was cash-in-hand arrangement with a foreign vessel owner – almost certainly Romero himself.

I shuffled back down the ditch and kept my head down until well out of sight of the gunpowder boat. I was now back at Thames Haven freight station. Luckily, there was no one about. Clearly anything of value must have long gone as there was no watchman to be seen. I knew there were no more trains today so set out on the four-mile walk along the track back to Rainbow Lane. It started to rain, and I could feel a blister starting to develop on my left foot. It was turning into that kind of day. Just mile after mile of featureless marshland with the occasional sight of passing boats to break the monotony. After an hour or so, I reached the point of the track, near to Rainbow Lane, where Fontaine had died. I could imagine the young lad, in the summer sun with a good sted under him. This would have been a marvellous playground for him, riding up and down the track, finding a good spot from where to sketch the boats on the river. The innocence of youth, his life robbed by hardened criminals who felt the need to silence him. These thoughts made his death even sadder. I doffed my hat in remembrance and set off up Rainbow Lane and then along the country lanes for another two miles before I reached Stanford-le-Hope village.

It was now almost teatime and the public house opposite the church was open, so I went in and treated myself to a pint and a pie. I slumped down in a seat opposite to the coal fire that warmed the snug bar. I felt exhausted, but glad I had witnessed with my own eyes the theft of the explosives and Frankland's involvement. What next?

There was no point rushing to inform the Customs and Excise, as the *River Plate* would be well outside British waters by now. So, in all probability the next time it would make land would be on the West African coast. Then straight from there to Buenos Aires.

So, there was little point in going to the Excise. The same was true of the military. I had no credibility with them now, being out of uniform for over twenty years, and making accusations against an officer with thirty years' experience in the army would in all probability be fruitless. No, my only choice was to take my findings direct to Scotland Yard and hope that they could liaise with Woolwich Arsenal and the Excise to bring both Frankland and Romero to justice.

At that I finished my drink and walked the last quarter mile downhill to Stanford-le-Hope station. Time to get home. Scotland Yard could wait until tomorrow.

SIX

Sullivan of the Yard

THE VERY NEXT MORNING I emerged from Westminster station alongside the Thames. This part of London had recently been redeveloped with the impressive new Victoria Embankment, and the building specially built for the police force, Scotland Yard, all within easy walking distance.

I made my way along the embankment and crossed over the road to Scotland Yard. I came to the front desk and asked for Inspector Sullivan. He was the contact that Hope had suggested in one of our early meetings. In no time Sullivan had come to the desk and introduced himself.

"Samuel Coleridge Sullivan, please to meet you, Mr Reeves. How can I be of service?"

"Thank you for taking time to see me. If you have an office we could go to, as the information I have is rather sensitive."

He nodded.

"Certainly, this way."

What can I say of Sullivan? The first thing was he was very young. Probably late twenties with jet-black hair perhaps kept neat by the use of Makassar oil. He was slim of figure and wore his police uniform well. He must have risen through the ranks very quickly.

We walked down the panelled corridors and entered his office. I took my seat on the chair opposite him. Between us was a fine polished timber desk with parquetry inlay. Before long I was at my ease and able to explain the detail of both my experience at Thames Haven and the possible link to both the city of London and Fontaine Hope's death. He listened intently. Finally, he spoke.

"I think Mister Reeves that we may be able to help you in respect of what you witnessed yesterday. I can certainly alert the Customs and Excise and the senior officers at Woolwich Arsenal. In respect of the other matter, the possible link to Master Hope's death, I am afraid we would need much more hard evidence before that matter could be progressed."

I was disappointed at this but felt I had done all I can.

"Thank you, Inspector Sullivan. I appreciate this enquiry involves not only crimes in London and Essex but also links to merchants in Argentina, so I appreciate this will be a difficult case. I can only implore you to do your very best as an innocent lad, Fontaine Hope, was, I believe, murdered and his grandfather is desperate to find the truth and bring the killers to justice."

Sullivan nodded.

"Very well, leave it with me."

At that our meeting concluded and I made my lonely way back to Whitechapel. I would dearly have loved to speak to Hope about all this, but he was still on the high seas, not available to telegram yet. I simply had to continue without his guidance for now.

And so, I waited, and waited. Every day felt like a lifetime. How would Sullivan handle this? I could not get involved myself being a lowly private detective. Would they be arresting Romero at his office near Fenchurch Street, organising the military to take Frankland into custody, telegramming West Africa in the hope of intercepting the *River Plate*? I had no idea.

Finally, after almost two weeks Sullivan contacted me by telegram and invited me into the yard late morning on the next day. I arrived early and after a short wait was led through to his office. He was sat behind the desk, and I could immediately tell that all was not well. He spoke in polite but restrained tones.

"Thanks for coming in, Reeves. Let me first of all say that we were very grateful for the information you provided. It has been very helpful and—"

"Have you made the arrests then?"

He almost sighed.

"I am afraid things have not gone too well. We arrived at the door of Romero's offices in Thames Street only to find that they were empty. Apparently, the day before he had disappeared and shut down the company overnight."

I was fuming.

"And Frankland?"

"He didn't arrive at the Arsenal for work. Seems to have left his wife and children and disappeared off the face of the earth."

I sat stunned and furious.

"How could this happen? Did somebody here tip them off? What is going on?"

x

Sullivan squirmed a little and finally replied, "I am afraid we have no idea how they got wind of what was to happen. All I can say is that we are using all resources to find these men and bring them to justice—"

"I don't suppose you have any idea where they might have gone?"

At this I stood up and walked out. Childish I know, but I had handed the police these men on a plate, and they had somehow fouled it up.

I swiftly walked out of Scotland Yard and immediately determined to take matters into my own hands. I strode to Westminster Station and took the underground into the city. In no time I was standing outside Romero's offices in Thames Street. Just as I had been told, they were empty, with no clues as to why, or where the company could be contacted. I stood around fuming for a few moments then spied a gentleman standing outside another business house smoking on a polished rosewood pipe. He had a grand stove pipe hat, not the more modern bowler, as younger city gents were tending to choose. He was carefully lighting the tobacco in the pipe's bowl and seemed at ease with himself and the world. I went over to speak to him.

"Excuse me but I cannot help but notice that Thames Haven Limited has moved. Have you any idea where they have gone?"

He was a middle-aged man who clearly enjoyed his tobacco, after a long draw on the pipe he spoke.

"No idea. Turned up on Wednesday morning and it was all shut up. Funny business if you ask me. Assumed the company were doing well."

"What about the staff? Any idea where they went to?"

He tapped his pipe again.

"Sorry, cannot be of much help to you on that. We do have one girl who worked for him who has just started with us though."

"Is it by any chance Miss Pound? Her Christian name is Elisa I believe. She worked for Mr Romero."

He smiled a little.

"Yes, she was wandering around here like a lost soul that morning so I suggested she could come to work for me instead, till things were cleared up. She jumped at the chance."

I was delighted by this news.

"Is there any chance I can speak to her?"

"I do not see why not, but she probably knows no more than me. She is on her lunch break now. In any case it might be better to leave it for a while. I think she is upset by the whole thing."

I thanked him profusely for his help. I knew where to go now. It was lunchtime and I would put money on her being at her usual place.

I strode off down the street and into the tearoom. Yes, she was there, and eating on her own, and in her usual seat at her usual table. I walked over and sat down on the other side of her table. She immediately stiffened; clearly, she found my presence awkward and frightening.

I spoke quietly but clearly.

"Miss Pound, I am so sorry to disturb your lunch, but I think I can be of use to you. My name is William Reeves, and I am a private detective."

She looked at me like a frightened rabbit in a trap.

"Excuse me, sir, but I just wish to eat my lunch alone."

She turned back to her cup of tea and gently lifted it out of the saucer.

"I appreciate that I am insensitive in disturbing your meal, but I have information about Mister Romero which you might find of interest."

She looked at me; her eyes had a sad look about them. Her scars seemed worse today as well, a deeper pink, bordering on red.

"Please go away."

"You must have been shocked when you turned up for work and found the offices all locked up and Mister Romero gone. I can tell you the background to all this. You must want to know how this has occurred."

She looked at me, and then around the café furtively.

"Mister Reeves this is not an appropriate place to discuss such matters."

At that she did something I was not expecting. She took a small notepad from her handbag and with a pencil wrote down a few words. She then slipped the piece of paper in my direction. I picked it up.

It had the words 'Meet me in the waiting room buffet, Fenchurch Street, five o'clock tonight.'

I looked at her, then nodded and left the tearoom and made my way home.

I spent the rest of the afternoon trying assiduously to work through my backlog of missing persons cases at home but with little success. My mind was totally absorbed by Elisa; there was just something about her that touched me.

I made myself look presentable and at five on the dot arrived at the buffet on Fenchurch Street station. I did not have to wait long. Within minutes she had arrived and on seeing me shyly walked into the refreshment room and stood beside my table, but not too close. I had already stood up and then pulled out a chair and when she was comfortable gently pushed the chair in. I sat down and tried to meet her eyes.

"I am so pleased you could come, Miss Pound."

She gave a cautious smile. I quickly ordered some tea and biscuits. I felt quite awkward. I decided to try and break the ice.

"Is this your usual station for your journey home?"

She did not smile but stared at the table. There was a silence, finally she said, "Mister Reeves, I very much appreciate your interest, but I have come here purely to find out a little more about what happened to the company, and Mister Romero."

I stuttered slightly.

"Of course."

I then slowly and precisely went through the background to my involvement and the occurrences on the marshes at Thames Haven. She listened intently but said nothing. The teas came. I tried to find out more about her personal history, she was reticent but then told me that she had worked for the company for five years and that she had been taken on because she could speak Spanish. She did not elaborate as to why she was bilingual, so I left it at that.

The conversation was very much one sided, with me leading but desperate to make it sound as if it was not an inquisition. Finally at six o'clock she informed me that her train to Barking left in five minutes. I enquired as to how long she had lived there but again she seemed unwilling to say much. In her disposition though was the hint of a smile. Perhaps a sign that she enjoyed my attentions?

As she stood up to leave, I found the confidence to say what I had been longing to but holding myself back from.

"Thank you, Miss Pound. Or can I be so bold as to call you Elisa?"

She almost smiled.

"Yes, of course, Elisa is fine."

"Thank you and I must say, Elisa, that I have very much enjoyed our talk. Perhaps, it would be possible to meet you again, same time same place, next Thursday so that I can keep you abreast of any new information I receive?"

There was a hint of a smile.

"I would like that very much."

She held out the daintiest of hands and I gently kissed her fingers. I could have sworn at that moment her complexion turned slightly red.

"I will see you here next week then, Mister Reeves."

At that she left the table, walked out through the door and headed for her platform. I stayed where I was, concerned that I could spoil the atmosphere and make her rethink her promise.

A few minutes later I left the station myself, and with a new spring in my step.

We carried on meeting, every Thursday teatime, all through the winter. I think for both of us it had become the highlight of the week. But it remained completely platonic. The signals she gave off made it clear that this was the way it was. Although superficially the reasons for the meetings were to keep her updated on the case, in practice there was little to report. The trail had gone cold. So, we just talked about her work, my work, anything really. I got the feeling that she was lonely underneath it all but her details of the life she lived outside work were sketchy at best. She was also very secretive about her past. I had assumed she was Spanish but then discovered she was actually from Argentina, hence the reason she was working for Romero. Beyond that things got awkward. It was as if everything that had occurred back in South America was off limits. The conversation always went dead if I pushed it, so after a while I never touched on this subject. However she did admit to living alone in rooms near Barking station– I had not been invited to her home yet.

She did have some interest in the whereabouts of Mister Romero but for my part I had little to report. There had been no sightings of him, or Frankland. The only clue was at the Royal Standard in North Woolwich, where I discovered on a visit that Mary Kelly had disappeared the same day as he did. From this I assume they went off together. No idea where, but the barman of the pub did remember that Mary had some family in Liverpool, so perhaps she might have gone there. I contacted Edward Hope, who was now back at his estancia in the Argentine, and explained what had occurred. His telegrams in return seemed pleased at the progress but disgusted at the police's ineptitude. He was more than willing to carry on financing me in my search for Romero.

Winter turned to spring. We were still meeting every Thursday at five. We started venturing out a little further, with walks down to the Tower of London to see the boats on the river. I was now at the stage where I could hold her hand and help her on with her coat, but little more. Any other show of affection brought on awkwardness in her. Gradually

I found ways of breaking through her cool exterior and finding something that lay beyond. I also started plucking up courage to ask more personal questions.

"Elisa. If you don't mind me asking, I have always admired your hair and dark brown eyes, and I know you speak Spanish and that you are from Argentina, but not much else."

I let the silence do its work. After a pause she answered, "There is not a lot to know. I was born in the Argentine, and then came to England. I am not that interesting really."

"So, how did you end up working for Alfonso Romero?"

I detected a slight wince as I said his name, but then she continued.

"Mister Romero invited me to come to England as he knew I could speak the language better than himself. He gave me a job in his office. After the long sea voyage it was difficult to go back to the Argentine, so I am still here now."

She looked around awkwardly, as if someone might be eavesdropping.

"My life just is not that exciting. Meeting you every week here is about the most exciting thing I do."

She smiled deeply. God she was lovely.

"Of course." I reciprocated her smile.

The conversation drifted along. She was a girl of juxtaposition – friendly but shy, clever but sometimes awkward. She seemed to indulge in the hobbies of a single woman: needlework and reading; she was also very interested in ferns and told me she had a collection of them back in her rooms. I would have very much liked to see them and to see where she lived but no invitation was ever forthcoming. Perhaps she was too good for me, and just saw me as a pleasant friend and not a potential husband? One interest she had, which was a little odd, was a belief in Spiritualism. She never mentioned this to me at first but it gradually emerged that she could not see me on certain nights of the week because of this. Once, in a moment of curtness, I dismissed the idea of life after death and being able to contact those who had gone. The look on her face was one of disgust.

"Clearly you know nothing about it!"

I was now in so deep that I continued.

"Please explain."

She took a while to answer, like a frightened rabbit her eyes darted back and forth to me, unwilling, or unable, to express her feelings.

"When you have lost people close to you the desire to see them again, to communicate with them, is overwhelming. It is that desire combined with the power of a great medium's that makes it possible to reach those on the other side. You have to have the desire to make contact, to believe it is possible. I have had many great tragedies in my life and lost many people close to me. That is why I believe, really believe, and it hurts me so much to see that you ridicule those beliefs."

There was an awkward silence. I tried to pacify her as best I could.

"You may well be right. After all I understand Queen Victoria herself often has séances at Windsor Castle, and these give her great comfort."

She chanced a look at me but was now clearly going back into her shell.

"That is very true, which is why I find your lack of belief disappointing. Perhaps it is best that I make my way home now."

She stood up. I could tell from her demeanour that she was hurt. There was clearly no doubt in her mind that Spiritualism was a genuine way of communicating with the dead, and that my attitude spoilt the whole atmosphere between us. There was nothing much more to say. All I could hope for was another chance to repair the damage my comments had caused.

We left to go to our own homes. I could see from her demeanour that she was almost in tears. I longed to hold her tight and make things right but this was not the moment. She walked off toward her train. She would be going back to her rooms alone and hurt. How much I would have loved to make things right between us, but sometimes things just do not go to plan.

We continued to meet though; perhaps she just put my beliefs down to ignorance. We soon had our own bench in Trinity House Gardens, where, on sunny spring nights, we would sit overlooking the tower and taking in the fresh smells of the new season, while studiously avoiding the hustle and bustle of endless horse-drawn traffic passing Tower Green, and heading away from the city.

And yet our friendship remained stubbornly platonic. At times I considered whether to propose marriage to her, but my instinct told me that this was fraught with danger. If she said no, it would be all over, and I would feel crushed. I was also well aware that I still did not know everything about her, which whilst giving her an alluring charm was also a danger. We only saw each other once a week. What if I found seeing her all day, every day, became tiresome? The whole situation was getting stuck in a rut and I had no obvious way of getting out of it and on to the next phase.

SEVEN

The Past Catches Up

IT WAS THEN THAT FATE played a hand. At the end of June, I picked up a copy of the *Illustrated London News* and found it was full of reports about Louis Napoleon, the Prince Imperial and heir to the Bonaparte dynasty, who had died in South Africa at the age of twenty-three. It appeared from the article that though he was just an observer, and not supposed to be anywhere near danger, somehow, he got involved in a skirmish and was hacked to death by Zulu warriors. His body was now being brought back to Britain on the ship HMS *Orantes* with a view to holding an almost state funeral near his home in Chislehurst, Kent.

This story immediately brought back to me my experiences with Marie-Anne, a lover of his father, Napoleon III, who himself had died back in 1873. I had a brief affair with her in 1871 and that relationship had still left a hole in my heart that was difficult to fill.

During the next two weeks I found myself constantly

daydreaming back to the all too short time I had spent with her in Gravesend and Dover.

A couple of weeks later the funeral arrangements had been made public. The prince's body was being brought from Spithead on the Isle of Wight to Woolwich Arsenal by boat, spending a night 'lying in state' there, before being brought to Camden Place in Chislehurst, where his mother Empress Eugenie still lived. The funeral date was 12th July and I decided to travel to Chislehurst to see it.

What can I say of that day? It seemed all the nobility of Europe had turned up to pay their respects including our own Queen Victoria. There was an enormous funeral cortege leaving Camden Place, just as I arrived. There was the Royal Artillery Band with muffled drums, in respect for the dead, escorting the coffin. A gun salute fired from Chislehurst Common, and the prince's body was on a fine gun carriage pulled by a large team of horses. It was about half a mile in distance, through what was usually the quiet village of Chislehurst, to the local parish church of St Mary's, but today the sides of the road were packed with spectators. I could not quite work out why so many people were lining the streets. After all Louis Napoleon was of a dynasty that was once Britain's sworn enemy. Perhaps the presence of the queen had validated the whole affair. Even so, at times I was reminded of the public executions in my youth; such were the number of people watching. Were there thousands of people in London so bored they would just go to any public event that was free, or did they really care about the young man who had died in a foreign country? Perhaps though I was being too cynical, it could well be that ordinary folk felt the greatest sympathy for the empress losing her only son at such an early age.

With great decorum the cortege moved through the village to the church and eventually the coffin was carried in. I obviously had no invitation, so waited outside along with many others. After what seemed like hours the funeral was clearly over and the mixed bag of European royalty, politicians and important people started to disperse. I was about to leave when my eye caught someone in the throng, shaking hands, bowing, and scraping to the great and the good. Although it was eight years on, I recognised him at once, it was Matthew Toulouse, former aide de camp to Napoleon III, and as nasty a piece of work as you could ever meet. After a few more moments of making his presence known, Toulouse stepped to one side; the crowd was thinner now, so it was possible for me to get over to where he stood. Why I wanted to speak to him, I do not know. It was just instinct. I stood in front of him and held out my hand. For a moment I could tell he did not recognise me, and then I could see he did.

"Well, if it isn't Master Reeves. What brings you here?"

I held his stare. "I just came to pay my respects. It is a tragedy the prince died so young."

He looked me up and down. He had hardly changed since I last met him, back in Gordon's office at Gravesend. There was still a meanness about him.

"I suppose what you have really come for is to find if I have news of your friend. You know the one who left you high and dry at Dover. What was her name? Marie-Anne, of course."

He gave a thin smile, and then continued.

"I am afraid I have bad news for you on that front. It seems she died last year. Probably from the pox, after all those years of being a courtesan."

I stood frozen to the spot. What a bastard Toulouse was.

"Of course, it was always likely to end that way. I gave you fair warning when I met you last, but you seemed so smitten by the whore, you did not take my advice."

If it had not been a funeral, I would have smashed his face in, there and then, but I held myself back. He could clearly see my anger.

"Well, it has been nice meeting you again, Reeves, but I have important work to be doing."

At that he turned and rejoined the throng of dignitaries, leaving me standing alone, bereft.

I turned and walked away, following the throng heading towards Chislehurst Station. Many of the people tried to engage me in conversation but I would have none of it. I had too much to think about. Was Marie really dead or was this another cruel joke of Toulouse's? Could I have done things differently eight years ago? Something that might have persuaded her to trust me with our futures? Why was I so upset anyway? Surely my future was with Elisa? Perhaps this sad event had turned my thoughts to maudlin nostalgia for a past that never was.

I trudged on and after waiting at the station for the crowds to disperse finally got on a train back into London. The time waiting had made me decide on something though, life was too short. I would tell Elisa my true feelings for her and not let her slip away like Marie.

EIGHT

Yes or No?

THE NEXT THURSDAY WE MET at five as usual in the buffet at Fenchurch Street. I was still very upset following the funeral and the information that Toulouse had imparted. She looked the same as always, tidy, shy, and oddly beautiful. Luckily, the weather was kind so I knew that a location away from the station would help.

"It is a beautiful evening; shall we go for a walk?"

She smiled coyly.

"Of course."

At that we stepped out of the station and slowly strolled down towards Trinity Gardens. Perhaps she sensed an awkwardness or sadness in me because she asked if everything was fine. I replied that it was but that I had something to ask her.

We finally reached the gardens and were pleased to see our favourite bench empty. I gently ushered her to take a seat and, once fully settled, sat down beside her. She looked at me.

"What is it, William? You seem so distracted today."

I tried to smile.

"I have to tell you that I went to the funeral of Louis Napoleon, and surprisingly it really affected me."

She frowned.

"But why was that? You did not know him."

I decided I would only tell Elisa half the truth.

"Perhaps it was because he was so young, just twenty-three, it made me think about how fleeting and precious life is."

She seemed lost for words. I did not usually talk like this; in fact I scarcely ever talked about my feelings.

"The truth is that I am very fond of you, very fond. We have known each other for a few months now, and I hope that feeling is reciprocated."

Again, she smiled awkwardly but said nothing.

"So, I am wondering, hoping, that you might do me the honour of becoming my wife?"

Silence. More silence. Finally, she stood up.

"I cannot. I cannot! Please do not ask me ever again. I am going to the station now. Please do not follow me."

At that she walked away, without looking back and walking as fast as she could. There was no point in pursuing her.

I was dumbstruck. Destroyed. I sat back down. I longed to follow her, but my instincts told me to give her distance. I was almost crying. After five minutes or so I stood up and made my way back to my lonely home. I did not sleep well that night. In fact, I did not sleep at all. In my thoughts I was constantly trying to tell her what I felt, but the words were never right. The night passed as I went over all I had done, and what I had done that was wrong. Could I put things right? Next day I determined to speak to Elisa again and try to persuade her that my love was real, and she had nothing to fear.

I steadily worked all day through the various missing persons cases on my books, but my mind kept on going back to yesterday's events. Finally at four I left my desk and returned to Fenchurch Street station. Just after five she appeared, heading through the main concourse towards her Barking-bound train. I walked over and stepped in front of her.

"Elisa, I must talk to you. We cannot leave things like this."

She stared back at me. Things were very awkward.

"Please, I have my train to catch. I cannot say any more. Please let me go."

"Not until we have talked this through. If I have to, I will get on your train and follow you home and stand outside your window all night. Anything to make you talk to me."

At this she relented slightly.

"Very well, but not here. Let us go for a walk."

At that, side by side, yet in total silence we left the station and walked along Crutched Friars until we reached 'French Ordinary Court' a narrow side street. She stopped and turned to me.

"William. You are a good man, and I am sure you mean well but I can never marry you. It is as simple as that. I beg you now leave me alone and find yourself a decent girl. Somebody worthy of you."

I stared incredulously.

"But you are my perfect girl. I want no other."

She looked hurt, confused, almost as if I had slapped her in the face.

"You do not understand, I am a bad woman. I have a terrible past. So terrible that if you knew it all you could never love me."

There was an awkward silence. Finally she spoke.

"I have never told you the story of my life because I was scared it would frighten you, but if you persist to question me I will tell you."

I was confused and a little frightened but knew she had to be persuaded to carry on.

"And what can you mean by that? I know you to be a wonderful woman. Good in every way."

She stared into my eyes and spoke quietly.

"I have never told you the whole truth. I know you do not like Mister Romero but I have to tell you, that… I was his mistress for two years. That is why he brought me to England and gave me positions in his office… please do not look on me with disgust."

Silence filled the air. I broke it.

"What happened to finish it? And why did you carry on working for him?"

"I was in a terrible situation. In a foreign country with a young son to look after. Who would employ me? How would I get by?"

I looked deep into her eyes. She was clearly bereft, broken. I had to find out more.

"I did not realise you had a son. You have never mentioned it to me."

"There are so many things I have not spoken about because I am so afraid you will hate me. Find me disgusting."

I tried to reassure her.

"Of course I would never feel like that about you. Tell me, what happened between you and him."

She stared at me.

"After about two years working in his office and being his… mistress, something occurred, it was all harmless but Romero did not think so. A pleasant man tried to take an interest in me. I pushed him away as I knew Romero would go mad if there was another man in my life but it was too late. He was utterly convinced I was seeing him and as a punishment took my boy, Frederico, from me. He sent him back to the Argentine without telling me. One day I came home and his nanny was at my door. Romero had turned up at the nursery and taken him."

I had heard enough. She looked utterly broken.

"Let me take you back to the station. I will see you onto the train. I am so, so, sorry for having to ask these things."

She was red faced, tearful, broken.

"He had left me a letter with his terms and conditions. My boy was being sent to the Argentine to be looked after by a good Spanish family. If I behaved myself while he was away and carried on working at the office, then eventually he would tell me where the boy was and let me contact him. If I left his employ or saw this other man again the boy would forever be lost to me. And that was that."

I gently put my hand onto her wrist. She was clearly traumatised.

"And that is the end of the story. I have spent the last few years living like a hermit. Not able to find new friends, lonely, isolated and still longing to hear from my boy. But nothing. That is one of the reasons I go to the medium. Just in case Frederico has died. I would like to know."

I looked at her with deep concern. She plucked up the courage to continue.

"The truth is you are my only friend in the world now. Mister Romero always promises to tell me about my boy, but never delivers. I know I am weak staying in his office but what else can I do? If I keep him close then perhaps one day he will tell me where Frederico is, and I can return home and meet him."

At that she turned and tried to walk swiftly back to the station. At that moment she let out a shrill scream. It was obvious she had turned her ankle and hurt herself badly.

I could feel her pain. I reached out and grabbed her before she fell to the ground. It was awkward but she was clearly in great pain.

"Please let me help."

I held onto her so she would not fall over. Suddenly, quite unexpectedly she looked into my eyes and for the first time I had hope. The moment came and went.

"Let me help you back to the station and onto the train at least."

"Why, why do these things always happen to me?" She was almost crying now. She had no option though other than to use the help proffered, and begrudgingly agreed.

Slowly she complied. I put my arm around her and mopped her tears with my handkerchief. We half walked, half stumbled, together back into the station, with me taking all the weight off her leg by holding her under her shoulder. We must have looked a strange sight. But by hook or crook we finally managed to get back to her chosen platform. I kissed the top of her hand. She turned to me and said the words I had always secretly hoped for…

"Please come back with me on the train. I don't think I can get home on my own."

I gently hoisted her up onto the footplate and through the door into the carriage, where she sat down awkwardly and made herself as comfortable as she could, I sat down alongside her. It was a small compartment designed for eight people, with four facing four, but today there was just me and her.

Within what seemed like seconds the smoke was rising from the train's engine and we were pulling out of Fenchurch Street. The train gradually gathered speed and went under a bridge so for a moment we were engulfed in darkness and the smoke from the engine, then out again into the open Then she said something unexpected.

"William. I am cold; can you put your arms around me?"

I duly obliged.

Then, almost without warning she kissed me. I wrapped my hand around her head and drew her towards me. We were kissing, I was ecstatic. She was crying. Really weeping but kissing me harder through the tears.

"William, you don't know how much I have dreamed of this."

And that was one of the most wonderful moments I have ever had. I was only too delighted to reciprocate her affection, it is what I had longed for all that year.

The journey passed with us clinched in embrace. I would kiss her all over her face, even her scars. This made her cry all the more. No tears of pain, tears of joy, perhaps relief that the wait was over.

Before we knew it the train had reached Barking. I would have gladly stayed on board, in this compartment, with her forever. I opened the carriage door and helped her out onto the platform. Luckily the street with her rooms in was not far away, perhaps a quarter of a mile distant. We slowly walked and she hobbled, out of the station, and down the street, holding each other tightly. Her grip was so strong, so passionate. In no time we reached the modest terrace house, where her rooms were.

I could see it was a small, two-storey house with a narrow dark hallway. Only really suitable for a single person. She had the ground floor to herself so clearly there must have been other tenants above. I sat her down, and then managed to light her gas lamps. The room, presumably the parlour, was a surprise in itself. On top of every available surface were ferns. She smiled.

"It is my hobby. Collecting ferns. If you go out into the yard there are even more. You can get there from the scullery."

I walked into her scullery and undid the catch over the back door. Yes, there were ferns everywhere in the narrow little back yard.

"Very impressive."

Then she seemed to come out of her trance and returned to the practical.

"William, if you could make me a poultice with a wet towel it might relieve my pain."

I duly obliged. There was something very satisfying and loving about wrapping a moist towel around her ankle. It was nice to see a little more of her legs as well.

"Why do you like ferns so much?"

She seemed happy at this question and smiled.

"Because they remind me of what I am, my life. I spend it in the darkness, in a cold office shut away but… all I need is a tiny ray of light to give me hope, to make me something else, and something better…"

I was listening intently; she did not often speak like this, from the heart.

"Do you think I could be that ray of light?"

"William, I hope you are. I really do."

At that we kissed, long and hard. I could feel the truth in her words. Somehow in the comfort of her home she was no longer the Miss Pound in strict office clothing, but a free spirit.

I knew this was my moment. Without hesitation I lifted her with one arm around her back and the other under her knees. Now I am not the strongest man in the world but somehow I found it within me to lift her out of the chair and following her directions through to the single bedroom. I laid her out on the bed. She gestured for me to join her. We kissed and embraced.

"Elisa, I have dreamt of this for so long. You have no idea."

We kissed again. Then I decided to go further and took off my jacket and began to undo my shirt. She was still in her clothes and had yet to make any move to remove them.

Then suddenly as quickly as it had began the atmosphere changed. She pushed me away gently but firmly.

"What sort of girl do you think I am? Some mollie you can sweet talk and take to bed."

I was stunned. For a moment I thought she was joking, but sadly, this was not the case. She rolled over in the bed so her face was away from me and pushed it deeper into the pillow.

"Please, I apologise if I have been too forward. I can assure you that I have the utmost respect for you."

She was quieter now but her words still cut deep.

"That is what all men say. Words, sweet as fine wine but all they want is sex."

She seemed strangely broken; in fact I suspected she was crying into her pillow.

"I can assure you my thoughts for you are honourable. I want to make you my wife. What more can I pledge than that?"

Silence.

I decided that I must persist. This chance might never come again.

"It is cold. Let me sleep beside you. I will not touch you if that offends. I will prove that it is love for you that I have, not some primeval lust. Please, let me stay."

There was no answer but I took that to be assent. So I did as I said and lay alongside her into the narrow cool bed. I did not sleep a wink. I was too excited, too overwhelmed at just being so close to her. After a few minutes, or it could have been much longer, I felt her hand touch my face.

"I am sorry, William. You are a man. With a man's needs. I know that you love me. If I am not too late, we can start again."

At that she moved over and spread herself on top of me kissing my mouth and face. Soon we had turned over so I was on top of her. It was the start of a long, magical, night. She was everything I dreamed she would be. Even her facial scars just added to her uniqueness, her real beauty and the long wait for this moment made it all the sweeter.

In the morning I reluctantly left her, so she could stay at home and wait for the bruising on her leg to go down. We both agreed it was just a sprained ankle and that hopefully she should be able to return to work in a few days. I would gladly have stayed with her in Barking all day, unfortunately I had already agreed a meeting with Bill, and could not really miss it.

Also Elisa seemed a little more distant now, as if last night had just been a dream from which she had awakened back to reality. Even so, it was with a heavy heart I left her and travelled back to the city.

I sat on the train feeling both tired and elated and sad. All and everything. Then as I thought more about her I reached into my jacket pocket and read through my notes on the case. It was something that Edward Hope had said to me, that I had probably forgotten. It took a few pages but finally found it. The nanny at George Hope's house in the Argentine was named Rosina and she suffered injuries to her face in the attack! I had a strange cold lump in my stomach. It couldn't be, could it? Was Elisa really Rosina? And, if so, why had she taken on an assumed name? This was when Hope and Romero were still business partners, so getting a position with that man would have been an obvious move. I was still torn though. Did she really have to be Romero's mistress? It made me physically sick just the thought of it. I wanted her all to myself. I wanted to be the only man who had ever made love to her.

This could easily end up as a can of worms. I closed my eyes and tried to think of my next action. How could I make sure she trusted and loved me when she found out the whole truth? I had no idea. For the time being my thoughts went back to the joys of the night just gone. By hook or by crook I must get her to believe in me. To trust me enough to become my wife.

NINE

New Leads

I MET BILL IN THE Lovat at noon. I arrived before him and was greeted again by that strange mixture of smells: fish from the market, sawdust, and spilt beer from the floor. This was obviously not an inn to frequent when you were cold stone sober. I also wondered if I smelt of her perfume. I had not been home yet to freshen up. I didn't want to. I didn't want to lose her scent on me.

Bill soon arrived, and the pints were going down quickly. The point of my visit was to pick his brain. Had he heard anything of Romero or Frankland?

He delivered as always.

"I expect you're wondering what, if anything, I have heard about Romero?"

I nodded.

"Well, you might be in luck. Rumours are coming out that he is connected to a shipping business in Liverpool. No firm sightings but lots of whispers about a swarthy Argentinean pulling strings behind the scenes."

This is what I wanted to hear. "Brilliant. Anything on Henry Frankland?"

He sighed.

"No nothing to report but as he wasn't in shipping my usual sources are not of much use."

"Seems like Mary Kelly at the Royal Standard also disappeared the same time as him. Some of the regulars said she had family in Liverpool."

Bill's eyes lit up.

"Well, there's an easy way to find her new address."

He gestured towards the barmaid at the far end of the bar.

"That is her sister. Romero's piece. She is still here."

I could have kicked myself, of course she would know.

"I'll see if I can get the address out of her."

Bill looked at me as if I were some innocent choir boy lost in the world of men.

"No, she will say nothing. There are easier ways to skin a cat. You have still got expenses for this investigation right?"

"Yes, Mr Hope is still funding me."

"Very well. Two guineas should do it."

He held out his hand and money changed hands. Then he swiftly and seamlessly slipped behind the bar. I could see him just speaking to a man in the corridor, leading perhaps to the upstairs rooms. A middle-aged man with an obscene purple, swollen nose, full of cracked veins, popped his head around the corner. That must be Kelly's old man. Within seconds Bill had returned with a slip of paper. He surreptitiously handed it over.

"There you are. Mary Kelly's new address."

I looked at the paper. It had written on it: 'The Weaver

Quay public house, Chester Bridge, Frodsham, near Liverpool.'

We both smiled. It had been as easy as that. Bill smiled knowing he had done the business.

"She still sends her sister birthday cards. More fool her."

We had a few more pints, Bill was always good company. Finally, it felt time to leave. I had already decided to travel to Liverpool. Perhaps I should have stayed in London with Elisa but I had to keep on with the job. Mr Hope had paid me good money and I could not let him down.

"Thanks for your help, Bill. I will let you know what transpires in Liverpool."

At that he surprised me. For a moment, his usual bluster disappeared, and he seemed younger and less sure of himself.

"Any chance I can come along with you?"

I was speechless for a moment, so he filled in the awkward silence.

"I have not been to Liverpool for years. There is lots of shipping people there that I've never met in the flesh. Be useful for me." I smiled.

"Certainly, if that is what you would like. I had always just assumed that the city of London was your neck of the woods, and you never left it."

"Even I can get tired of the same faces, the same pubs."

I could only agree but with Bill you felt that banter was the requirement of the day.

"You know what they say? Tired of London, tired of life." He smiled.

"Maybe there is some truth to that."

We then sorted out arrangements for the trip. This had

been a turn up for the books. Once sorted, I bade farewell and set off home. I had to prepare for the visit. I was bound for Liverpool and with a new companion on board.

TEN

The Mine

Henry Frankland surveyed the scene in front of him. Only he was no longer known by that name, he had now taken on the pseudonym Nathaniel Drover. The people at the mine knew no better, they knew nothing of his real name, his past. They would not have cared anyway. He was just another 'know it all' Londoner telling them how to mine for salt.

What can we say of this mine? Well, it was deep, that was for sure, and very new. The workers were blasting through the geological layers at speed with limited knowledge of the topography and precious little understanding of the dangers of this type of work. Henry had a rudimentary knowledge of using explosives in a mining situation, but that was enough to get him the position of chief engineer. It was all about getting the salt out as quickly and cheaply as possible. If a disaster occurred and they were to hit an underground river, or suchlike, the mine would simply be abandoned and a new one found. As for the men, most were Irish in any case.

Henry had little love for them and was not too concerned by injuries or fatalities to these men. They were reasonably well paid and knew the dangers. This was man's work. His role was simple. Decide on the location for laying the explosives, set the fuse, stand back, and hope for the best. Mining by this system saved time and money in digging by hand, and there was a ready source of explosives to hand. Anyone could have done this job, but Romero had trusted him, had given him another chance, so he owed it to him to make it work. Also, there was serious money to be made. Salt was wanted everywhere, particularly in the new canning industries in Newfoundland, the demand for it overwhelmed supplies, so everyone was making a killing. The days of surviving on his army pay were now a memory. This was a risky life, but a well remunerated one. This mentality affected the whole of the undertaking. The miners wanted the maximum pay in the shortest period of time, the bosses wanted to get the salt out and onto boats before the bubble burst. Everything was on the cheap. A minimal number of candles wedged into the walls to light the scene, underfed pit ponies dragging the salt carts, precious little health and safety. Henry did not know what he was doing, his cursory understanding of geology barely sufficed and often mines were dug into the wrong places, missing the salt seams. The explosives were also hit and miss. Usually, they used old-fashioned gunpowder for blasting, as the new nitro-glycerine was hard to come by, and tricky to use. The gunpowder made more noise and dust than it was worth, and it was then up to the poor overworked miners to dig the salt out by hand.

So, what was in this for Henry? Firstly, he had Mary Kelly back at the inn at Frodsham. Though it was difficult to tell, she seemed to care for him, and she was certainly much keener on sexual favours, and very experienced, which made a change from his previous frigid wife, who he had left back in Silvertown. There was also the hope of big money. That would not come just from the wages that Romero paid, no, the money would come from deals on the side. Creaming off salt and selling it separately, not through the books. It would be that cash-in-hand money that would make his fortune. This thought warmed him as he laboured through another dark day in the cool underground cavern.

ELEVEN

Liverpool Bound

TWO DAYS AFTER OUR MEETING in the Lovat Arms we were Liverpool bound from Euston. Bill was a good travelling companion, constantly telling tall tales and anecdotes featuring people I didn't know. He was a strange man in many ways, unmarried, but worldly wise, weary but at times almost childlike in his enthusiasm. It was difficult to know what Bill you were going to get. Even away from London he still seemed to have that mad cockney humour which clearly attracted the female sex and charmed old ladies. I was still at a loss to know his background but gradually a picture emerged. He still lived with his mother, who was now a good age, in Catford, South London. He had been in the world of shipping since the age of fourteen and now had thirty years' experience – hence he owned his own company and was able to take time off to accompany me. Wine, women, and song were clearly his weaknesses, but he had somehow avoided ever being wed. The said wine, or in his case usually beer, had led to a fast-expanding waistline and the beginnings of a red nose and double chin. All in all, though, he was good company.

The train took us north, firstly through the shire counties then on to the industrial heartlands around Birmingham. It was easy to see this country was now divided between the rich and poor, the townspeople and the country folk. Birmingham seemed just a mass of chimneys and grey/black smoke and, underneath it all, mean terraced houses. An hour later we went through the potteries around Stoke, and this was scarcely better. Endless tall chimneystacks sprouting from red brick factories. Finally they gave way to the open countryside of Cheshire before coming to our destination at Runcorn. The station was just shy of the magnificent new railway bridge that spanned the river Mersey. It would have been nice to travel over it but our destination at Frodsham was closer to Runcorn than Liverpool.

Luckily, we had travelled lightly with just a pair of travelling cases between us. We were also pleased to see a hansom cab available for hire just outside the station. We quickly boarded and agreed with the driver that he would take us to the best hostelry for overnight stays in Frodsham, near the river Weaver, which was somewhere called the Kings Arms, just off the Chester Road bridge.

The ride from the station to Frodsham was also instructive of the sort of country England had become. To our right, the river Mersey was stacked full of shipping with canal boats and Mersey flats entering the river from the Bridgewater canal. To the south were steeply rising hills which appeared to be in use as a kind of giant quarry. I consulted my trusty pocket atlas and suspected that we were looking at Runcorn Hill, one of the biggest sites for excavating red sandstone. I noticed that the tracks of the tramway, presumably taking sandstone from the quarry to the river docks, actually went straight across the road. The cab driver seemed nonplussed by this and carried on regardless. Clearly small trains crossing the road were just another minor inconvenience to be avoided. Beyond that we passed through some unspoilt countryside for a mile or so, before descending to the plain on which sat the river Weaver itself. This traversed much of Cheshire before entering the Mersey just south of Weston village.

Coming towards the Chester Road bridge we could see the open flat country to the south, bounding the Weaver, whilst at the bridge itself a multitude of business had sprung up, presumably to service the river trade. A number of Mersey flats – the local boat which bore a great resemblance to the barges on the Thames – were sailing downriver. My understanding was that they were probably carrying salt.

Tucked in the middle of these new industrial buildings was a single inn. I could see its name on the fascia above the door 'The Weaver Quay'. So, this is where the Kelly girl had gone, and by the look of the passing river traffic it was probably a busy place serving the bargees and flat men that worked the river.

Our chosen hostelry, the Kings Arms, was just a hundred yards' distance from it and was more suitable for gentlemen travellers – or so the cabbie thought. We pulled up outside it, thanked the driver, and paid him. We then went into the inn and arranged a room for the night. We would be sharing, both the room and the bed. Hopefully, Bill would not get too drunk. It was now early afternoon. Rather than go to our room we decided to visit Kelly's pub. Even as we approached it on foot, I got the distinct impression that it was a rough place, as a drinker – clearly worse for wear – was being thrown out the front door! The riverside inn was squeezed in between a narrow road that ran parallel to the Weaver, and the riverfront itself. It was surrounded by the riverside wharfs and warehouses and dark timbered buildings that towered above it.

We walked into the Weaver Quay. I could immediately understand why the cabbie had been so negative about the place. It had a dirty air to it and was full of hard-faced bargee types, men who worked the river and worked it hard. The smell was one of unwashed bodies and damp clothes, which the sawdust floor did little to pacify. There were no women in the inn at all apart from the lady behind the bar, and I recognised her at once as being Mary Kelly. It seemed prudent that she did not see me, so I found a half decent table in the corner while Bill went for the drinks. We were soon sat down together grateful for a pint of ale despite the dirty atmosphere. As we drank, we could hear snatches of conversation from other tables and from the men propped against the bar. Several of them were trying it on with Mary; men seemed to swarm around her like bees round a hive. Or should I say, flies around shit. But perhaps I was being harsh.

Virtually everyone in the inn seemed to be connected to the salt trade in some way or other and the majority were boat people who had moored up close by. There was no sign of Henry Frankland and the sign above the door stated that the licensed victuallers were Nathaniel Drover and Mary Kelly. I wondered if Drover was his new nom de plume.

Bill was already thinking ahead.

"I asked Mary if Mister Drover was in the house today. She said he was still at the mine but would be in later."

I smiled; I knew it must be him.

"Well, I suppose he does know a lot about explosives. I would not fancy working with him though."

Bill obviously had an idea.

"I think one way of finding out what is going on would be for me to meet him. He might remember you, but I doubt if he will have any idea of who I am. I'll arrange to have a business meeting with him tonight, and make it clear that I am a rich trader looking to get hold of cheap salt for my business in Newfoundland. If I know that man, he will want to do a deal, cash in hand. That might give us some clues to where Romero is operating."

I agreed wholeheartedly. Bill then went back to the bar and arranged with Mary a time when Drover would be around so they could talk about a business opportunity. I always admired Bill's attention to detail, in asking her he flirted just a little to let her know he found her attractive. That was the best way of keeping girls like her sweet. By the time he had finished it was smiles all round.

Bill returned to our table.

"It is all arranged. Told her my name was William Dickens and that I was looking for a cheap, ready supply of salt. Cash paid, no questions asked. She almost bit my hand off."

I smiled. Bill knew what he was doing. We left the bar and made our way back to the Kings Arms.

TWELVE

Salt of the Earth

That evening Bill set out on his task. He walked to the inn by the river, leaving me sitting alone at the bar of the Kings. Before long, my thoughts turned to Elisa. What was it about her that had gripped me? She was certainly an enigma masked in a mystery. Why was I so absorbed and infatuated about her? I knew so little about her yet so many things in her life were a constant: the same meal in the same tearoom by Fenchurch Street, every day. The same train home. Even working in the same street. Which also begged the question: why did she carry on working with Romero after what he did to her? The more I thought, the worse it got. I was missing her. Missing the sense of routine that she gave to my life. In fact I was wondering if leaving her was a wise move after all. I had got so far, after so long, and here I was two hundred miles away.

Meanwhile Bill was now inside the Quay and had spotted Frankland, behind the bar. He went up and shook his hand.

"William Dickens pleased to meet you, Mister Drover."

Frankland looked him up and down. He was clearly tired but had his confidence boosted by a few free drinks and the thought of Mary later on that night.

"Mr Dickens. What can I do for you?"

Bill smiled.

"Word is that you might have access to a ready supply of cheap dry salt. I have a financial interest in a canning factory in Newfoundland and we are constantly on the lookout for reliable sources of salt. At the right price of course. Can you help me in that direction?"

Frankland looked him up and down.

"From London are you? I can tell by the accent. I assume you have heard that all the finest salt is from Cheshire and the best ships to Newfoundland sail out of Liverpool."

Bill nodded.

"Indeed, that is the case. I have come here because I have been told this is the place to find good quality cheap salt."

He seemed content at this.

"I dare say I could help you with that. But I need to know you are a man of your word. Any deal between us would be strictly cash up front. And remember the demand for our product is unquenchable, so I do not need to do business with you."

"So, what are the arrangements? How does it work?"

"You pay me for a certain amount. So many barrels. Then you organise a boat – a fifty tonner Mersey flat would do – to come down to our wharf at Northwich, at a time that I fix. Pay up front, load the barrels onto the flat, and the deal is done. What you do with them after that is your business."

Bill had to think quickly.

"What sort of set-up have you got then? What if I was to buy the salt and you transport it for me to Newfoundland. What sort of cost would that be?"

Frankland was now less happy at the direction things were going in but any money-making opportunity had to be grabbed with both hands. Mary had expensive tastes. He got out a pencil and a sheet of paper and started scribbling on it. After a couple of minutes, he handed the paper to Bill.

"Here you are. That is the sort of cost for shipping, obviously dependent on how big the order is."

Bill looked at the figures and feigned concentrated interest.

"So, who is your shipper? You cannot be doing all this on your own."

Frankland looked peeved at this turn of events. Clearly this London guy was no fool...

"Of course, I have a legitimate shipping company on hand. We can guarantee that the cargo will be delivered safely, and on time."

Bill had the answer to this.

"No offence, Mr Drover, but I've seen too many ships wrecked along the north Wales coast or holed by the rocks off Anglesey. I need to know you have a reputable shipper with good ships and experienced crews."

For a moment Bill thought he had lost the momentum. Frankland almost ground his teeth in impatience at this cheek.

"Alright, but keep this to yourself. We usually use 'Black Star shipping'. They have fine offices in Liverpool. You will not get safer or more reliable carriers than them."

Bill smile inwardly. Got you.

"Thank you. I am very interested in your offer. I will get back to my office. Make a few calculations then let you know. I bid you good day."

Frankland was less than pleased he had not clinched the deal there and then but let it go. After a shaking of the hands Bill bade farewell and walked back to the Kings.

Bill arrived back and recalled the events of the evening. I was pleased with the outcome and said so.

"Thanks, Bill. It looks as if his greed will be his undoing. I would put money on it that the 'Black Star' line is a front for Romero. There is no way that stupid old soldier would have all these connections without him. He is just an old engineer who has never left Woolwich. No, Romero is at the back of all this."

Bill nodded.

"What is the plan then?"

"First thing in the morning we go to Liverpool and check out the Black Star offices."

Bill concurred. We had a nightcap then slept well. Or as well as good be expected with Bill snoring and farting alongside me.

From Frodsham to Liverpool is only ten miles away, as the crow flies, but as there are no bridges over the Mersey till you get to Warrington a further ten miles to the east, we decided on a compromise which was a cab to Runcorn station then train to Liverpool Lime Street.

The cab arrived at eight o'clock and before leaving we took in the scene on the Weaver, which was flowing strongly towards the Mersey and sea beyond. A number of Mersey flats were clustered close to the jetty of the Weaver Quay. There was clearly much activity and numerous men making the boats ready to sail, but only one took my eye. Yes, it was Frankland in the midst of it all. Barking out orders. The flat that he was on had thrown its tethering hawser onto the bank and was moving away from the jetty towards midstream. It was soon obvious that the boat was heading downstream towards the Mersey.

We got into the cab. So, could he be going to Liverpool? If so, what were the chances of him going to the Black Star offices? This had been a stroke of luck. We carried on our way and caught the train from Runcorn towards Liverpool, crossing over the Mersey on the new Britannia railway bridge, which spanned the river majestically.

Arriving at Lime Street we got another cab to James Street where we soon found a suitable hotel. We chose it because it was within view of the Black Star offices across the road from it. The porter, an old man by the name of Fred Dobbs, seemed like a good chap, albeit he had the eyes of someone who has seen it all before. He gave us a room at the front of the hotel on the second floor overlooking the street. We left our bags there and walked across the road to the shipping offices.

Just crossing the road was a danger in itself. I was amazed at how busy Liverpool was. I had always assumed it was a provincial city, but it was buzzing with business. The streets were full of horses and carriages and carts and constant movement. I was immediately taken by the gulf between extreme poor and the rich shipping merchants. Tramps and Arabs, horrid little ragged children, seemed to be hidden around every corner and they were clearly light fingered, so the visitor needs to keep his wits about him.

We walked past the offices and very grand they were. A fine new three-storey brick-built edifice with imposing doorway and brass sign for 'Black Star' alongside. Immediately beside the offices was a pub, The Star of the Seas which appeared to be an old coaching inn, as it had stout timber doors at the side, leading to an area where horses could rest and feed, and be fussed over. Meanwhile the coach passengers could take refreshments in the pub. I wondered if it was still in use for those purposes.

We returned the few steps to the hotel from where we could sit in our room and, through the front window, view the comings and goings at the offices.

It was now late morning and there were few visitors to the offices. No sign of Frankland. But then just after noon our patience was rewarded. The Star of the Seas opened its doors and one of its first customers was, yes, you have guessed it: the man himself. We both had the desire to go inside the pub to confront him but stayed back. Twenty minutes later he emerged. Interestingly he looked up and down the street, almost as if he feared being watched, then set off down towards the docks area.

So, he had come to Liverpool, but gone to the inn, not the offices, unless there was a linking corridor between them? Presumably, he had done some business, perhaps with Romero himself, or one of his underlings. We were still none the wiser.

Bill was clearly getting bored by mid-afternoon. I knew that being patient was part and parcel of my job, but Bill was of a different school of thought. I suggested he visited some of the local alehouses to pick up any titbits about the Star of the Seas pub. My only condition was that he went via the post office with a telegram for Inspector Sullivan of the yard.

Needless to say, he jumped at the idea of visiting the local inns.

I carried on with my observations. The afternoon wore on. Finally, around four some action occurred. A cab pulled up outside the Star of the Seas and the cabbie got down and tapped the door adjacent to the yard entrance. Within seconds the high timber doors opened and the cab entered the yard area. Frustratingly I could not see into the yard itself from my viewpoint. Within a minute the coach and horses departed. The opening to the passenger section of the cab was closed by the shutter blind, so I had no idea who was inside. The cab swiftly made progress. It was heading east. Away from the city centre and the docks.

Was Romero inside that coach? Is this how he had become invisible?

I relaxed from my surveillance and rested, awaiting the return of Bill.

It was past seven before he came back which was disappointing for me, as I had been waiting to eat. Clearly, he had numerous pubs under his belt.

The hotel did not have a dining room so we walked the streets till we found a restaurant nearby.

Bill went straight for the main course and clearly had some tale he wanted to tell me.

"So, Bill, have you gleaned any useful information on your travels?"

He could not wait to impart the news.

"I sniffed around, basically asking where I could find some good mollies. Just for a bit of entertainment."

I scoffed. And…?"

"I got various tips but then one chap told me in passing that a lot of the really classy mollies went to the 'Star of the Seas', and this is the interesting bit. They get taken to some Spaniard's house, on the outskirts of the city, for parties."

He sat back knowing full well this could be the clincher.

We finished our meal. I was keen that Bill should not get too acquainted with the large glasses of red wine that he seemed to drink like water.

We set off back to our hotel passing the Star on the way. It was fairly quiet tonight. I turned to him. "I thought you said it would be full of mollies. It looks dead in there."

Bill huffed.

"That is tomorrow night. Saturday is party night. That is when the action happens."

We passed by the pub. The temptation to go in was strong but I was minded that being recognised could queer our pitch.

We entered our modest hotel, and I was pleased to see the porter was still up. I took my chance.

"Fred. Can I pick your brain?"

He almost smiled and moved the clay pipe out of the side of his mouth for a second.

"You can try."

"Between you and me, we are getting a bit bored. Too much business not enough play. Do you know what I mean?"

I let the words hang in the air. Bill got the gist and carried on.

"Rumour has it that some quite tasty mollies can be found in the pub across the road. Any truth to that?"

Fred took his time to answer. He tapped out the loose tobacco from his pipe.

"You gentlemen are right to say that mollies go there. Bit of a problem though. The best mollies do congregate there. Usually around eight on a Saturday night, only problem is… thing is a rich gentleman has them put into cabs and sent to his house in the sticks. That is what I've been told anyway."

I was interested, he knew more than I thought.

"So, what time does the cab leave from the pub?"

"They usually have a growler or two, get at least six girls in each. About nine o'clock."

I slipped a crown from my pocket and gave it to Fred.

"Thanks, Fred."

He looked a little worried.

"Of course, I've only told you, so you don't embarrass yourself. I think the big knob that organises all this would not be best pleased if you went over there and creamed off his girls. If you get my drift."

We both nodded. I turned to Bill.

"I think I'll call it a day then, get an early night."

Bill looked both shocked and mystified.

"It is only eight o'clock. The night is still young. I'm going down to the docks to see what this Liverpool place is all about. You are coming, aren't you?"

I knew what he meant but I also knew that the night would end with him picking up some cheap Irish colleen and exchanging money for whatever. I did not want any of that. I was missing Elisa badly and to go with Bill would have seemed like treachery.

"No. You go on your own. I have letters to write."

Bill snorted.

"Very well. I will see you later."

At that I went up to the room and Bill disappeared into the night.

I spent the evening writing some more of my letter to Elisa, I just could not get her out of my mind. Perhaps it was my feelings for her that made me so sure that avoiding the dubious nightlife of Liverpool was the right decision. Also, I felt awkward at the way that we, as fairly affluent Londoners, would take advantage of poverty-stricken women reduced to prostitution. Bill appeared to have no such scruples.

It was past midnight before Bill reappeared and woke me up. We then passed another disturbed night. I was getting too old for staying in strange hotels with even stranger men.

Next day it was fine and sunny. Bill seemed fine. Clearly late nights and too much drink seemed not to affect him. He just always looked the same. Like a tired old hound dog.

We made our way down to the Liverpool police station. I had contacted Sullivan of the Yard before leaving London and he had telegraphed his opposite number in Liverpool. Our local contact was a Detective O'Connell. Luckily, the man was in, so we were sent straight to his office in Dale Street. O'Connell seemed a decent enough chap, a bit older than I had expected, with big grey mutton-chop sideburns and knowing eyes, but clearly well abreast of the crime scene in Liverpool. I explained that we had heard a rumour that a wanted criminal, Alfonso Romero, might be living just outside the city and that we were aiming to follow a group of mollies who were taken there on Saturday nights. He seemed to take it all in. I told him that as we were unsure about this that it was best not to have police involvement at this stage;

however, if our hunch were correct then we would hope that the Liverpool police could raid his house the next day.

He went along with all this and wished us well. We left; at the door, Bill turned to me.

"That guy O'Connell, he has got a side to him. Best not tell him too much in the future."

I looked genuinely surprised but also concerned. Bill's gut feelings were not to be dismissed lightly.

We then went to a cab yard, which O'Connell had recommended, and hired a growler – a four-wheeled Clarence – we also paid for the services of a driver who was willing to work that evening. Having completed the transaction, we arranged for the cabbie to meet us at eight thirty outside the Star of the Sea.

Dead on time the cabbie turned up, we took our seats inside surreptitiously, and waited. Before long, a number of giggling mollies appeared. It was obvious what their trade was, even at a distance. We watched them go inside the Star and waited some more. The cabbie seemed okay as he was being well paid for doing nothing. Finally, about nine the huge timber gates to the courtyard were opened from the inside, and a coach appeared, turning left along James Street, perhaps heading out of town. We could just hear the talk coming from inside their coach, which was also a four-wheel growler. Female voices. After a few seconds the heavy courtyard doors were shut and I bade our driver to follow the coach immediately. They had a hundred-yard start but we were soon shadowing them from a distance. They made steady progress in a south-easterly direction, and we were soon out of the city. There was now a mix of fine houses in large plots, many recently built. The cobbles gave way in places to more rural, dirt, roads as we hurried along. The night was getting cooler, and I could see the steam coming from the horses as they hurried along. I could see from the sign by the road that we were now at somewhere called Moseley. At this point the growler in front turned left up a minor road which went uphill between attractive trees silhouetted in the moonlight. To our left now was an eight-foot high wall, made out of sturdy red stone, the walls seemed to go on forever. Whatever was behind them must be something significant. The road narrowed then doglegged to the left. I could now see the stonework in the thin moonlight was pitted with green moss, so deduced from this that it was north facing. Abruptly in front of us, but luckily a good hundred yards away, the coach slowed down to a stop with the driver shouting 'whoa' to his pair. I urged our driver to stop as soon as possible. He did this. Hopefully, we had not been seen. The wall had a set of high gates inlaid and alongside a small cottage, a gatekeeper's cottage perhaps? I could see the gates being opened for the mollies' coach. So, this must be journey's end. I turned to Bill.

"What do you think?"

He replied without hesitation.

"Follow them through. The gatekeeper will just assume we are a second coach full of mollies."

Bill stuck his head out of the carriage and instructed the driver to follow them through. He also promised him a big fat tip if he would do so. The driver replied without hesitation.

"No problem, sir."

He immediately got the team going again. By now the front coach was halfway through the gates so we were just out of sight. Our driver sped up. The gatekeeper was now standing by the outside gates ready to close them when he saw us coming. Our driver knew what to say.

"Second helpings of mollies tonight for the boss."

The gatekeeper seemed content at this, and we manoeuvred through the open gates.

Once away from the gatekeeper I bade our driver to slow down to a stop. Ahead some way, and half obscured by a fine Cedar of Lebanon tree, was an imposing manor house and, in the drive, in front of it, the first coach unloading its cargo. There was much chat and giggling, and the sound of walking over the gravel drive as they hurried in out of the cold. Clearly this was work the girls liked. Or at least they were making the most of a bad job.

I dismounted from the coach and Bill followed. Then handed our driver two guineas.

"That will be all for tonight. You can go back to town before the gateman shuts you in."

The coachman doffed his hat.

"Very well, sir. It has been a pleasure."

At that he gently manoeuvred the carriage around, and retraced his route.

We were now alone in the grounds of this massive house. We initially hid behind the Cedar tree and watched proceedings. All the girls had left the coach now and the driver was taking his team back out. Presumably, they had agreed a time for a pickup later on. Or perhaps in the morning, I had no idea how these sorts of parties worked. We watched the horses and coach pass by us, the driver intent on the road ahead and getting back into town and making more money as soon as possible. The gatekeeper let him out, then himself walked back towards the house. He passed not ten paces from us but seemed oblivious. He was an old man and hopefully quite deaf. We waited a little longer. I was clear on our mission. We had to witness that the man who lived in this mansion was Romero himself. Once this information was obtained, we would simply report it back to Liverpool police who would take over. I had not quite worked out how to get out of the walled garden, or how far it was walking back to the city, but those were details for later. I turned to Bill.

"Alright. We just need to see him. Confirm it is Romero, and then disappear. Hopefully, we can do this without drawing attention to ourselves."

Bill nodded. He pointed to the side of the mansion. It looked as though it was possible, from what we could see in the darkness, that all four sides of the house could be reached from the grounds and that the main entrance could be avoided.

We crept closer to the house. We could hear vague sounds of laughter and partying. My guess was that copious amounts of drink would be flowing to get the girls, and probably Romero, as well, ready for the main course.

There was no sign of any security to speak of. Hopefully, Romero believed his eight-foot-high walls were his defence against the outside world. Gradually, and at a distance, we slipped around to the back of the house. From there we could see a fine gothic style picture window, probably at the end of their main hall, and beyond that, light and laughter. The room was clearly magnificent with a centrepiece of an enormous chandelier which lit the room up with its gas lighting. We both stared intently. Then Bill nudged me and pointed. Yes, there was no doubt. It was Romero, standing by, of all things, a grand piano, one hand holding a glass of wine, the other a laughing mollie. I almost wanted to shout with joy. I looked towards Bill expecting him to be ecstatic as well but the sight that greeted me brought a chill to the pit of my stomach.

A man stood with a revolver, pointing straight at Bill's head. A second man now touched the back of my head. I guessed he also had a revolver fully cocked.

"Do not move, gentlemen." A steady voice stopped us dead.

"I don't know what you are doing here but you had better have a very good excuse. The gentleman who owns this house values his privacy, and intruders, like you, will get short shrift. Now move. This way."

He prodded me in my back and pushed us towards an innocuous entrance door at the rear of the mansion. I had no idea who these men were, but I knew they would kill us on a whim, so did not resist.

We were led through an open back door and into what looked like the gardener's storeroom. I noticed now, in the thin light from a kerosene lamp, that the men were hooded so I could not see their faces. They gestured for us to sit down on the tired wooden seats. We duly did. Within seconds the door to the main house opened. I recognised the man who came through immediately, it was Alfonso Romero. His features were unchanged – a big head, nose, low forehead with a shock of jet-black curly hair. His head looked as if it came straight out of his torso, bypassing the neck, which was the sort you would find on a hardened prize fighter.

"You two!" he snapped, and then to the hooded men. "Go through their pockets."

We sat silent as this frisking was carried out. Meanwhile another lamp had been lit, giving the room a strong but eerie light. Romero looked at the contents of my jacket pocket. The thought hit me – bugger, it was my letter to Elisa, still not posted. He tore open the letter and silently read its contents. He smiled wryly. Sucked the air out of the room and spoke.

"So, it is William Reeves, Private Detective, that I see before me. And if I am not mistaken Bill Barrington, a man more used to drinking in London bars than breaking into law-abiding people's homes in Liverpool? Pathetic."

I noted his Spanish accent had weakened and he spoke good English.

"So, what are you two doing here, skulking around in the middle of the night? Surely you are not going to arrest me for some misdemeanour?"

I decided I must speak.

"Mister Romero, I am fully aware of your involvement in the dynamite trafficking out of Thames Haven, and that you have gone into hiding because of it. I came here to ascertain that this was your new home and will advise the police accordingly."

He laughed.

"You will advise the police! Why should they be interested in the affairs of a decent hard-working businessman? The biggest international distributor of salt in this city. I know nothing of this dynamite nonsense you talk of."

I was not letting this go.

"I think you know full well."

He looked at us almost pitiably.

"So, what have we here? A London small-time shipping

agent and a tuppenny halfpenny detective, who, from this letter, looks as if he has an infatuation with one of my ex-staff, Miss Pound. Truly pathetic."

He was not finished.

"I knew Miss Pound when she was younger. She was smitten with me, but I rejected her. But I can see, from this letter, my cast-offs are now entrancing you."

"This has nothing to do with you!"

"Mr Reeves, I suspect this has got everything to do with her. Nobody up here is interested in a bit of bad business I did in London. This city is full of real crooks. Sailors stabbing other sailors every night of the week, Catholics cutting up Protestants. Husbands beating their wives to a pulp. The police up here have real work to do here. I am a respectable businessman. In fact I often have members of the Liverpool constabulary coming to the little parties I hold in this very mansion. A party that, incidentally, I am missing because of your interference."

I looked at him sternly.

"You will not get away with this, no matter how well connected you are."

He had clearly had enough. He turned to his minders.

"Blindfold them and take them away to our little holding cell. The cold one. I will decide what to do with them later."

At that he left the room, presumably returning to his party. We were swiftly blindfolded and led away. These men were strong and well-armed so resistance would have been futile.

We exited the same way we came in. I could feel the slight change in temperature and a breeze on my face. They pushed us across what I assume were the lawns until after a minute or so the feel of grass underfoot changed to the crackle of leaf mould and twigs in woodland. Then we stopped, a heavy door was opened. I could hear the hinges squeaking. Then unexpectedly I was pushed hard in the back. There was nothing in front of me at all. I fell, I don't know how far, but ten feet at least before crashing into a solid stone floor. I could hear Bill beside me had also had the same treatment but seemed to have come off worse as he was yelping in pain.

I could hear the heavy door slam shut behind and above us.

THIRTEEN

Cold and Lonely

THE SHOCK OF THE FALL had loosened the blindfold, and I was soon able to wriggle it off and look around me. I knew immediately the sort of place I was in. It was an icehouse, but thankfully almost empty of ice, just some sludge on the floor. I could see little else as it was almost pitch dark, just some odd shapes above me hanging from a beam, which stretched the full diameter of the structure, near the top of the icehouse. The shapes were small animals; rabbits maybe, hung up in this cool place to keep fresh. Aside from that it was a typical icehouse, brick walls maybe twelve feet deep with conical sides sloping slightly outwards but impossible to climb with your bare hands.

I could just see Bill beside me, he seemed in pain.

"Fell on my ribs. I think they may be broken."

I had no idea what I could do to help so I just put my arm around him.

"Don't worry we'll get out of here and get you fixed up."

My words sounded hollow, even to myself. I looked

around in desperation. The brick walls were just too steep to climb, we were in an impossible position and cold with it. The rabbits were obviously stored here because the temperature was so low they did not rot, but that same cold was no good for my bones, or for Bill.

We both sat down as best we could. Luckily, there was no ice residue, so we were not soaking wet. For a few minutes I spoke to Bill about anything and everything to try and take his mind off the pain but eventually I gave in, and before long fell into a restless, cold sleep.

I slept fitfully, waking at times to this cold nightmare. Bill was clearly suffering and hardly able to sleep at all. I kept looking up through the very dim light available at the tapering brick walls – was there any chance I could climb up them? Probably not. Things were getting desperate but I must have somehow nodded off again.

Sometime later I awoke. There was now some thin light coming through the cracks between the icehouse entrance door and its frame, a sure sign that this icehouse had not been used for its original purpose for some years. It must be morning, though the light was very thin – icehouse doors always faced north to keep the sun off them. Then a terrible thought struck me in the cold pit of my stomach. What if Romero was to go after Elisa as punishment for my investigation into his affairs? Fear and anger boiled inside me. I turned to Bill, who was also wide awake and looking ill and distressed.

"We have to get out of here. Nobody is going to come and rescue us."

He stared at me and nodded.

"If you can stand underneath the door, I will try to

climb on your shoulders and see if I can reach one of the hanging rabbits."

He obeyed my instructions. Despite his injury he was able to hoist me up, even though he was clearly in great pain. I scrambled to keep my balance on his shoulders, leaning into the brick wall and scratching a finger hold in the lime mortar joints. Inch by inch I raised myself up. Normally I would not have the strength for this, but I had somehow got within me a steely determination not to fail. Bill was beginning to hurt badly but I carried on. Stretching out, I could just reach the legs of a hanging rabbit. I thought there was precious chance it could take my weight but amazingly it did. From somewhere I got the strength to hang on and drag my hands up its carcass until finally getting a grip on the iron hook itself. With my last piece of strength, I swung towards the door, a few inches at first, then further, gradually working along the timber beam, which I prayed would take my weight. I was now a foot or two away from the ledge on which the door was located. Finally, I got myself onto the ledge and almost exhausted pulled off one of the unused hooks which were in situ waiting for the next rabbit. I noticed there was blood all over my hands, clearly the hook had gone right into my fingers, but I did not care.

I grabbed the hook, which thankfully was a sturdy affair, perhaps eighteen inches long, and used its end like a jemmy to open the door. This was not that easy. Icehouses usually have big heavy doors, and this was no exception, but after a few minutes of swearing and cussing the door frame cracked and the door was prised open.

Outside it was morning and the sun shone brightly. The sky was rich blue, and the greens of the trees and lawns had never seemed more beautiful. I should have been scared but I was not. All my joy was in having escaped from that dark hellhole. I looked around, nothing. No sign of life. My hand was bleeding, but I did not care. I stumbled away from the icehouse, my legs deadened by the night of cold and damp, then walked as quickly as my stiff legs would carry me to a canopy by the back door of the house. A ladder was hung up against the wall. I took it and returned to the icehouse and lowered it down to Bill. He struggled to climb it with his dodgy ribs but eventually was out. It looked like he might need a hospital visit. I looked around again. Still nobody. It was as if the place was deserted. We needed no more invitation and headed to the main gates in the perimeter wall of the estate. There was no sign of the gatekeeper. To my surprise the gates opened easily, and we were soon walking along a narrow country lane. Within a few minutes we bumped into a local, a man taking his dog for a walk. He saw our predicament and took us back to his house then after a cup of tea and some kind words took us down to the nearby railway station from where we returned to Lime Street. From there we got a cab to the main police station where the surgeon was called to look at Bill; he also bandaged my wounded hand. As I suspected his ribs were probably broken so needed more treatment. After more tea and biscuits, we returned to our hotel, exhausted and shocked by the experiences of last night.

I had left a message for Detective O'Connell, telling him about where Romero lived and our experiences from last night, but he was out on site with another case. Later that day O'Connell turned up at the hotel and reported on what he knew. The long and short of it was that his officers had just been to Romero's property in Moseley Hill and found it completely deserted. Somehow he had moved house overnight, but as to where, the detective had no idea. He took his leave. I wanted to return to London that afternoon but felt I should give Bill at least one night's good rest so decided to wait until the morning.

FOURTEEN

Back down South

NEXT DAY WE SET OUT for Lime Street and caught the express train back to London. Bill would need more treatment. I would need to make sure Elisa was safe. We left Euston and went our separate ways. Though I was glad to be alive I still had this awful feeling in the pit of my stomach that not all was well.

I had planned to get a hansom cab straight back to my rooms in Whitechapel but decided instead to look in at her office, just to make sure all was well. The cabbie worked his way through the heavy traffic of the busy city, the horses working up quite a sweat as the driver pushed them hard, and as per my request dropped me off by Fenchurch Street station entrance. No sooner had I stepped out of the cab than I had the feeling that something was wrong.

Outside the tearoom, where I had first spoken to Elisa, was a policeman brandishing a notebook taking down details from a clearly frazzled staff member. I walked over and tried to eavesdrop. I caught a few words but was still unsure what had occurred when the policeman closed his notebook and walked away leaving the manager of the tearoom, who I knew was called Louise, standing looking most upset.

"What has happened?" I implored.

She looked at me. I think she recognised me, but I think she would have told her story anyway.

"Just this lunchtime. One o'clock it was. That nice woman who comes in every day, Miss Pound, just sitting there reading her paper, minding her own business. Then…" She paused to get her breath. "Then these thugs came in. All masked they were. Two of them. They grabbed her and had her through the door and out into the street. Then, it got worse. I could see them push her into the back of a covered wagon. Then the driver cracked the whip and the horses raced away. It was all over in a minute. Shocked I was. Poor Miss Pound. Who could do this? She did not have an enemy in the world. Always so well-mannered and pleasant. And this being a respectable establishment catering for the city folk. I do not know what the world is coming to."

At that she returned to the safety of her teashop.

I was left standing aghast and broken hearted. So, Romero, or some of his thugs, was out for revenge, and they had got here before me. I kicked myself. I should have protected her.

The one person I cared about in the world, and her one great fear and hate, Romero. And now he had her in his clutches again. I felt sick to my stomach.

The rest of the day was a whirl of pointless activity. I reported the event to Sullivan at the Yard and he promised to give it a high priority. Bill was also clearly upset but had his own problems getting over the pain of his broken and bruised ribs. I felt very alone.

I returned home to my rooms in Whitechapel and waited, and waited. Nothing. The street outside was full of activity, busy with wagons and hackney cabs running back and forth to the city, but all I felt was emptiness.

What was Romero's game? Why did he want Elisa? Probably to give me a bloody nose, but beyond that?

FIFTEEN

Hostage to Fortune

Elisa lay on a hard stone floor. She had slept fitfully, or not at all. She was in a bare room with brick walls and no windows, some timber boarding and the remains of a curtain rail marked where one had been. She was hurting, all over. Something had happened. Why was she here? She moved from supine into a seated position and saw immediately that her wrists were bound in chains. Heavy metal chains that had already chaffed her wrists. She was cold. The room felt damp, almost fetid. There was no clue as to where she was. She listened intently. Nothing. Then a faint noise of birds in the distance, seagulls perhaps? It felt like she must be out in the country there was so little noise, perhaps a farm? Maybe with this damp and seagull calls she might be somewhere near the sea, or on the marshes. Her head was hurting. The last thing she remembered for sure was being dragged out of the café by two men in hoods and bundled into the back of a covered wagon. Then they travelled for miles, maybe two hours had passed before the wagon stopped, and blindfolded, she was taken out and brought into this house, building, room? She was no longer gagged so could at least breathe. She called out. "Help. Help!"

Finally an answer of sorts came back. The heavy timber door to the room opened and there before her was a man she had not seen for so many years. He had aged, and got uglier with it, but there was no doubt. It was the father of her child and once her husband, Pedro Diaz. He stared down at her. She looked back at him in disbelief. This made no sense; they were not in the Argentine. How could he be here? What did he want?

"So, Rosina, or do you like to be called Elisa these days? Such a pretty English name. Like a virgin would have." He smirked. Elisa spat back.

"What do you want of me? Why are you here? What is going on?"

He gave a greasy smile. What had she ever seen in him?

"The less you know, the happier you will be. For now let us be clear, you are my prisoner and we are in the middle of nowhere. Suffice to say Mr Romero is very irked by your friend Mister Reeves constantly poking about in his affairs. So much so that he will be told that he must keep his nose out, or something bad will happen to you."

"But what are you doing here in England? How did you know where I was?"

"Mr Romero knows everything. You worked for him long enough to know that. I have been working for him as well. But out of sight. On the marshes at Thames Haven, a night watchman. Nobody was interested in me. I was a nobody. I didn't even know you were in England as well, until he told me."

Elisa felt utterly forlorn.

"So what is to happen to me?"

"I am just following orders. You could be here for some time. It will be unpleasant for you. A damp room, poor food, no daylight… but I could make it more bearable. With your cooperation and agreement."

"What do you want?"

"What Romero has not told me is something you know. That is where our son Frederico is… you must know, and if you tell me, I can make things nice for you during your stay."

"I don't know. I have no idea. I think he is back in the Argentine. Romero knows more than me."

At this Pedro flew into a rage and grabbed her neck, holding it tight, threatening to choke her.

"Don't give me that."

"It's true. Has he not told you the full story…?"

He released his grip.

"Or does he just tell you what you need to know?"

Pedro's nostrils flared, he was angry alright. Elisa thought that sharing some information might calm his temper.

"The truth is Pedro that I did come to England with Frederico. And he lived with me for the first year. Then I fell out with Romero. As a punishment he took him away from me and gave him to someone else, someone in the Argentine, who became his new parents. But I don't know who that is. He just would not tell me. He said I was a bad mother, could not look after him on my own, that he would be better off with someone else. I had nothing to argue with. He owned everything of me. I had to keep working for him, keep on keeping up appearances. He even told me that eventually, if I behaved myself, I could meet my son again. Then I realised that what he meant by behaving myself was sleeping with him. Doing everything he wanted. It is him you should be angry with."

Pedro stood for a moment, seething, then went out the door, slamming it behind him. The air was filled with his anger.

And so a routine emerged. The bare floor was replaced by sacking for a bed… Three meals were brought during the day, a chamber pot and bowl and jug for washing were left in the room. It was Spartan, hard, cold, damp and unpleasant but survivable. Then on the seventh day, probably – there were no clocks or daylight to gauge the passing of time – the routine changed. Pedro brought a nice outfit in – blouse, skirt, hat, shoes – something typical of a good London clothes shop, and asked her to put it on. She did so, albeit all on her own struggling to get it right with no mirrors to help. She was also given some rudimentary cosmetics: blusher for her cheeks and lipstick. Then the door opened and for the first time that week she left the room which had become her prison and was shown into a parlour. Standing in front of her there, to her shock, was Romero himself and alongside him a man who was obviously a photographer. She was asked to sit in front of the hearth holding today's newspaper in front of her. She quickly remembered the date. Romero smiled.

"I hope your stay here is not too arduous, Elisa. If I can get assurances from Mister Reeves to stay out of my business you can be on your way in no time. For now this is just to prove to the idiot that you are under my care, and I can do anything I want to you."

His voice had a threat laced through it. Pedro stood nearby saying nothing; clearly he was still on Romero's team. The photographer knew to keep his mouth shut and say nothing. Within a few minutes the scene was orchestrated. The photographer took some pictures and hastily tidied his gear and departed. Romero was clearly not in the mood for talking.

"Take her back to her room, Pedro. She doesn't look too bad. You have done a good job. I wouldn't want Reeves and his detective friends to think we were harming her."

He smiled again, and nodded. She was returned to the room which was now her cell, and had to remove the pretty clothing, and go back to her single outfit that she had worn all week. It felt humiliating, but she was a realist. It was true Romero and Pedro could do what they liked to her. They could kill her and throw her body into the deepest river with lead weights around her feet, never to be seen again if they so wanted. She was helpless.

SIXTEEN

The Long Search Begins

Two days later a letter was delivered by the Royal Mail. It had been posted in the city of London and my address was printed. Inside was just a single sheet of paper. A photograph. It was a picture of Elisa, holding a newspaper *The Times* so that the date could just be read with a magnifying glass. It was dated just two days earlier. The photograph was a formal portrait with Elisa dressed in a nice outfit – similar to the office clothes she was wearing when abducted – seated in an unremarkable room, probably a parlour. She was not smiling but clearly following instructions because of the angle of the newspaper. On the back of the photograph were printed the words:

'Reeves. Keep your nose out of my business and Elisa will stay safe.'

Just that. No clues as to where the picture was taken. The London postmark told me nothing of any use.

I sat down. It took me a while to gather my thoughts. So this was it, Elisa had become his hostage and his bargaining chip to keep myself and the police at a distance.

I pulled myself together and quickly made my way to Scotland Yard to see Sullivan. Luckily he was available and I showed him the picture.

"Well, Reeves. There is not much to work on here. It looks like a normal house which could be anywhere. No marks to tell us who the photographer was. No clues at all really."

He sat back and for a few moments there was silence between us. Then he came up with something.

"The only thing is… there is a just a chance we might be able to identify the type of photographic paper. We have a new department at the Yard we call forensics. They can take a look at this. Don't think there is any likelihood of fingerprints but if we can find the make of paper that might point us to where the photographer bought it."

I smiled for the first time in a while.

"How many types of paper are there? How many shops sell it?"

"Sorry, Reeves, I've no idea on that one. But it's probably worth a try."

At that the meeting closed and I went home to await the outcome of the tests.

SEVENTEEN

Paper Chase

A WEEK LATER I WAS called back into the yard and was sitting opposite Sullivan again.

"Well, Reeves, unfortunately it appears that this type of paper is widely used; however, there are not that many shops that stock it. I had my lads look through *Kelly's Directory* and there are only a handful of places that sell it. The biggest one in London is 'Francis Ridgeway' at Chancery Lane – they seem to provide the materials for most of the capital's photography studios. So they might be worth a visit."

Sullivan handed me the photograph of Elisa back and the meeting ended. On my suggestion though he agreed to come with me to the photography shop. Within minutes I had hailed a cab and was heading towards Chancery Lane with Sullivan.

The shop was indeed a large affair with all the latest modern devices in photography, cameras for all occasions. I could see immediately by the literature that it was studios that were their main customers. Few normal citizens could afford the paraphernalia to take and develop photographs. Sullivan spoke to the manager at length and finally I was privy to their sales ledger with lists of paper sold and to who and when. It was a long list. However one thing did come to my attention: the list included so called 'travelling photographers' with no fixed studio. I questioned the manager.

"I noticed on the list a few photographers with no studios. How does that work?"

The manager was a kindly middle-aged man with greying hair. He spoke quietly but clearly.

"These people are a dying breed. The more cameras are about the less they are needed. Mostly they have their own wagons with all the gear on board and visit poor areas where there are no studios."

I pressed him for more information. He clearly had a wealth of knowledge.

"For instance, this chap I know does a lot of work for the gypsy community. Goes to their weddings and what have you."

He pointed to a name on the list. 'H.R. Scrivener of Grays, Essex'. "The giveaway is that his address is just a Post Office Box, so he is probably always on the move."

I was interested.

"So how does he work, do you think?"

"It's a simple system really. People like him come up to town and buy their various materials from me, perhaps once a month, and then they go wherever the work is. Surprising the number of gypsy camps in Essex and Kent, and at this time of year, what with weddings and the hop picking coming up, he is probably doing very well for himself."

I thought quickly. It was a long shot but perhaps it might be someone like Scrivener going to a house somewhere and taking the picture. Cash in hand, no questions asked. Safer than taking Elisa to a high street photographic studio.

We bade farewell to the manager and left with our notes of names and addresses of people who might be of interest.

EIGHTEEN

Dead Time

A WEEK LATER I ARRANGED to meet Bill at the Cheshire Cheese. Sullivan of the Yard was clearly doing what he could but nothing was coming to pass – no leads, no idea where Elisa was being kept – assuming, that is, that she was being held hostage against her will. I needed Bill's nose for trouble to find a way out of this pit of silence.

It was Monday lunchtime and the inn was busy, thankfully Bill was his old cheerful self, the broken ribs clearly forgotten; it seems it was not a break after all. We talked about nothing in particular for a while then I outlined the progress or lack of it to date. Bill took a deep sip of his bitter and after much thinking spoke.

"I don't know where you go from here, nothing obvious comes to mind. This Scrivener bloke, the mobile photographer, have you met him yet?"

"Tried to, went to his Post Office Box but it is just a tobacconist's shop in the middle of town. The owner would tell me nothing. Finally admitted that he turns up now and again without notice, picks up his post, pays the rent for his box when that is due, then disappears. Doesn't even have a regular time or day. Would not give me his home address, tried to pretend he is always on the move, of no fixed abode. I don't buy that."

Bill seemed deep in thought.

"You say that he does photographs for the gypsies. Maybe the way in is to get to know them. See what they know."

I scoffed at this.

"They are even more secretive than Scrivener. I don't know any gypsies. Do you? In any case I am sure they would be tight lipped, so what is the point?"

Bill was not put off by this.

"There is something that could get you closer to them. I was down the Lovat last week. Now some of Romero's old chums still drink there. So I was listening in. It appears that this Thursday there is a big prize fight out on the marshes somewhere east of Tilbury. Big name fighters and it is the gypsies that organise it."

"But that is illegal. Everyone knows that the prize fighting is against the law."

"Come into the real world, Reeves. Just because somebody says it's not allowed means nothing, especially to the gypsy boys. They have their own rules, their way of doing things. Anyway the long and short of it is that next Thursday you buy a train ticket for Benfleet and get the six thirty train from Fenchurch Street to Southend, via Tilbury. Somewhere en route you will be told where to get off, where to go. Likelihood is that the gypsies will already have the ring set up along with entertainment and bookmakers. It's all done by word of mouth. Some big toffs are going as well, proper city businessmen. People who think of themselves as gentlemen. They love a good fight and it being illegal makes it all the more fun to them."

I stood amazed at this. Prize fighting had been illegal for over twenty years, I had no idea it was still occurring.

"Prize fighting! I thought that went out with the flintlocks."

"You try telling the gypsies that. As long as there is big money to be made, it will carry on. They just have to keep it quieter, let punters know about the fights by word of mouth only."

"Very well, Bill, then I think we need to be on that train."

Bill smiled; this was just up his street.

"I will arrange it all."

I couldn't believe it was so easy.

"Anything we should take with us on the night?"

Bill smiled.

"Might help to have a hip flask, everyone will be drunk by the time we get there. The only other thing you need is to keep your wits about you. If they smell something funny, that you are not one of them, or worse still, that you might be spying for the police. It could get nasty."

The lunchtime rolled on. I knew that going to the fight was a very long shot but it was a possible toehold into the world of the gypsies and perhaps that might give me an idea about how to find Scrivener. I had no other leads to follow.

We left on good terms and walked back to the station to get a train home. I still had another option, which was to stake out the tobacconist's shop in the hope Scrivener might appear but that might turn out to be a waste of time. In fact my interest in this mobile photographer might easily be chasing up the wrong tree but it was all I had to follow at the moment, and something, some instinct, told me that he was involved.

So it was Thursday evening at quarter past six that I met Bill again at Fenchurch Street. We both perused the other customers at the station. There were a few more people worse for wear than normal but nothing unusual. We bought our return tickets and made our way onto the platform for the Southend train. Still nothing odd, though perhaps more men than usual in a party mood for this time of night.

We stepped onto the train and were in a compartment of ten seats, five each side of the aisle facing backwards and forwards. By a stroke of luck of lady and her child came onto the train and so there were only four people, including ourselves, in our compartment, which was a relief as we did not want to make polite conversation with anyone else going to the fight. Just before the whistle was blown a man walked alongside the train and seeing us spoke quietly.

"Anyone going to the party. Get off at Low Street." We nodded. The lady looked perplexed.

The train was soon pulling out of the station amidst the flurry of dark smoke billowing as it went under the Minories. I turned to Bill.

"Strange. This train is not scheduled to stop at Low Street; it's just a halt from my memory."

Bill nodded. We then spent the rest of the journey making polite conversation with the woman and looking out of the window admiring the sunset over the marshes, to the south side of our train. It was now possible to hear noise from the adjoining compartments and it was clear that a number of men were already inebriated and noisy with it.

By the time we reached Tilbury Riverside, dusk had fallen. The train came into the station then backed out so those seated facing forward now faced the other way. The journey continued for another five minutes and then the train slowed. Bill passed me the hip flask.

"Here, have some of this. You will need it to fit in."

The train came to a halt gently and I could see through the window a little used timber-decked platform with the words 'Low Street Halt' on a metal sign at its edge. We bade farewell to the lady and her child and stepped off the train. This was not a scheduled stop so clearly the railway crew must be in on it. Within seconds dozens of men had piled off the train. What struck me then was how well dressed they all were. I had assumed that a fight in the middle of nowhere would have attracted the scum of the earth, but these were mostly well-dressed city gents. Many with top hats and some with the more fashionable bowler hats, above proper city black suits. The train did not tarry long and immediately set off.

Soon the noise was building. Shouting, swearing. These were city gents, no doubt by the look of it, but they were all pretty pissed already. In fact some took the opportunity to relieve their bladders alongside the platform. Bill noted a few odd looks coming our way and swung into action by bellowing out to one and all.

"Where the fuck are we going? I hope we haven't got to walk miles…"

The words were spot on. The crowd immediately recognised Bill as a kindred spirit. I was trying to act a little drunk but failing badly. A man at the front end of the platform holding a railway lantern now took charge.

"Alright, everyone, it's only a furlong or so, to where we are going, just follow me and keep your noise down. And remember the train back comes at half nine. If you don't get it, tough, there will not be another that stops here."

At that everyone seemed to calm a little. There were maybe forty of us stumbling around in the semi dark following the man with the lamp. We were soon on a well-trodden footpath that led through a copse or small woodland. At the end of it was a clearing full of light and noise.

As we walked into the clearing we saw a surprising sight. In the centre was a boxing ring, set up on the grass, surrounded by lanterns on high poles. The whole place was a hive of activity with boxers and their seconds preparing for the fight to come, beyond that, and arranged in a horseshoe shape, were perhaps twenty gypsy caravans parked up with their tight decorated entrance doors facing towards the ring. We could see all this clearly because the area was ablaze with light. Bonfires were everywhere. There was entertainment as well, a man doing a fire eating act, another looked as if he was swallowing a sword. Bookmakers, with lamps strung above their pitches, were very prominent and clearly doing a trade. A large tent, or rather a marquee, was also well lit with a rudimentary bar and bartenders inside dispensing drinks from big pottery flagons. This was clearly a big, well-organised event. I wondered how long it was going to be before the performing bears turned up!

Bill, always in character, made a beeline for the bar. Considering we were in the middle of nowhere it was well stocked and we were soon deep into pints of porter, drunk from china mugs. Conversation and the shouting of the bookies filled the air all around us. One or two people recognised Bill and shared some perfunctory greeting, nobody knew me but by now everyone was too drunk to worry about that. In addition to the city gents there were also some very dodgy looking people hanging about, whether they were the fight promoters, security or just old-fashioned pickpockets, I had yet to find out. Also, surprisingly, there were some mollies that had clearly been shipped in as part of the entertainment for the night. There was no doubt of their calling; you can almost smell a mollie before you saw one. I can only surmise that for a price they would take you into the woods for some slap and tickle. I spoke to Bill about my impressions of the event, and he concurred with me. Basically most of the men here were either scum trying to make the maximum money at the expense of the punters, or were lambs to the slaughter, about to get fleeced, one way or another.

We played along with it all, Bill making numerous bets before drinking copious ale and porter. For a while I thought this was all going to be a total waste of time. Then I saw two things of interest, almost within a minute of each other. Parked up just beyond the last caravans in the crescent was a black covered cart upon which were inscribed the words 'HR Scrivener' – photographer, so, the man himself was here, presumably he had come to take pictures of the action.

The fights went on and on but I could feel a sense of excitement brewing. Finally it all came out. A new fight was starting soon and the two pugilists had entered the ring. There was a sense of excitement verging on awe in the air.

The referee stood in the middle. The emcee stood alongside him to introduce the boxers. He shouted, "And in the left corner, a man you all know and love. Undisputed champion for the last twenty years, Jed Bibby!" His voice reaching a crescendo. A man, built like a brick shithouse but clearly now over forty, stood flexing his muscles and staring out his opponent. Bibby had thinning but still dark brown hair, greased back. He was a good six foot tall, probably fifteen stone and clearly a man that could take, and give out, punishment. The announcer continued.

"And in the other corner, the challenger John Grief." This man went through a similar ritual to Jed, flexing muscles, staring at the opponent. Then a spit in the ring to finish things off.

The fight commenced. It was bruising. I spoke to the man standing next to me who I know had come up from the city.

"Why is this guy Jed Bibby so adored? Is he that good?" He looked at me with disdain.

"Jed is one of the greatest. The gypsy king we call him. He was a champion in the great days of prize fighting when you got crowds of thousands. Call yourself a fight fan if you did not know that."

Bill looked at me with a why-don't-you-shut-up face. The stranger continued.

"There is a lot of serious money riding on Jed. This crowd will push him over the line. He can't be allowed to lose."

Before the fighters started the bout they photographed together by Scrivener who was using a lime flash to capture the image in the darkness. Presumably he could not photograph the action as the artificial light would blind the boxers. I assume he was taking photographs of the boxing for publicity materials for the next event, as everything about this was illegal. In the dark I could not really see much of this elusive photographer. Older than I thought he might be, maybe fifty with dark hair and heavy mutton sideburns turning grey. Fairly undistinguished.

I took that in and got back to watching the action. There was little in it but the bare fists were taking a toll on both the boxers with black eyes and blood beginning to seep from the noses and eyes. There did not seem to be much between them. I don't know what the purse was for this bout but whoever won it, deserved it.

Then the real prize. From the corner of my eye behind me I saw a man come out of one of the caravans down the short flight of steep steps then across the grass towards the ring. He pushed a few punters out of the way to get himself the best vantage point. Even in the half-light, I knew who it was. Romero! He was walking alongside a man who was clearly well thought of in the gypsy community by his clothing and bearing.

For a moment I wanted to run over and throttle him, make him tell me where Elisa was being held. Bill saw this and immediately put his arm in front of my chest and pushed me into the shadows. I blurted out, "It's him, Romero. Let's give him a taste of his own medicine."

Bill looked at me like a father figure.

"You and whose army? We are outnumbered a hundred to one. If we attack him we are probably dead or badly hurt at least. Let us just watch for a while."

"Who is the man next to him?"

"That is Medlock Lee, the top man in this camp and probably joint promoter of the fights with Romero."

So we kept our eyes on the fight and it was clear all was not well for Jed. He was taking a beating. Whether age was catching up on him, or the opponent was better than anyone expected, this fight was only going to end one way.

Blood was flowing now from a cut over Jed's left eye, a deep one. The referee started looking towards his corner at the seconds. They stood their frozen, unwilling or unable to throw in the towel. Then they looked over to Romero as if awaiting an order. The order was clear. He was to fight on… he did so.

In the midst of this mayhem a young girl, probably no more than nine, tugged at my sleeve.

"Lucky heather, sir. Get your lucky heather and fate will always be kind to you."

I stood unsure what to do, Bill had no such qualms.

"Sling your hook."

The girl melted away looking for more amenable punters no doubt.

We turned our attention back to the ring. Now it was truly brutal. The older man was knocked down, and then staggered to his feet before being knocked down again. The blood was so abundant; he and the referee would soon be sliding over the floor. The seconds looked again at Romero; still he urged them to force Jed on. It was pointless of course, I doubt if Jed could even hear the noise from the crowd, or his seconds. He was a dead man walking.

Then another drama started playing out. A woman approached Romero from behind and started shouting in his ear and shaking him. What the hell was going on? Our fight fan next to us soon put us straight.

"That is Jed's wife. Rose, she's given Romero a right earful. Wants him to get the seconds to throw in the towel."

We kept looking at the massacre in front of us. I did not want Romero to recognise us. Now the gypsy woman was tearing at his hair. She was probably about forty herself, tall and slim with wiry jet-black curly hair and an almost Latin face with piercing black eyes. Romero did not budge but soon fate intervened. Jed was now flat out on the floor. Looking half dead and clearly incapable of rising to his feet, let alone fight. John Grief was announced as the winner by a knockdown and his hand was raised to the sky by the referee. It was all over.

The seconds carried the prostrate Jed from the ring back to the caravan. He was clearly a difficult carry as he appeared to be a dead weight. Rose went with him into the caravan. Romero seemed to have disappeared altogether. From the atmosphere I guessed that many punters had lost a lot of money betting on him.

We looked at each other. What the hell was that about? Surely a prize fight should have some rules, some mechanism for stopping if one of the pugilists is getting pummelled.

We spent much of the rest of the night trying to keep a low profile. Bill asked one drunken punter if he knew who the top man in the gypsy camp was, he confirmed that it was a guy named Medlock Lee. He also knew that the Spanish man, presumably he meant Romero, was the money behind all this. But that was all he knew.

We went over to watch the remaining fights but the atmosphere was already going flat. Clearly the defeat of the gypsy king was a hard pill to swallow. The prize fights carried on but the atmosphere of tension never really left this strange place. I could soon understand why this bare-knuckle boxing had been made illegal. Every punch seemed to draw blood; I think one of the boxers even lost some teeth, as something shot out of his mouth onto the floor. Any fighter showing signs of weakness would be pummelled into the dirt. Needless to say the punters loved all this. It was blood sport of the highest degree. Some of the pugilists looked past their best. Perhaps they had been fighters, like Jed Bibby, when all this was still legal and they got crowds of thousands back in the fifties. That seemed a long time ago now. Clearly there was serious money to be won by the victor, the losers at best could only go away and lick their wounds. That's if they could walk away at all. It would not take much bad luck for one of the fighters to be killed in that ring.

Whoever won the fights seemed to make no difference; there seemed to be running arguments with the bookies over every result and a generally sour atmosphere.

In between bouts the entertainment was mostly drinking, watching the fire eater, and avoiding the pickpockets and whores. One man running a stall had a tank full of eels which on request he would pluck out of the water and cut into segments on a chopping board with a massive butcher's knife. The eel's blood ran into the water tank which was now red in colour. The eel was then thrown into a pot of boiling water hung over an open fire for cooking. He was doing a roaring trade, as the endless drinking was giving the punters an appetite.

Now and again the noise of drinkers and the shouting and boasting and bragging was interrupted by a fight breaking out. Two city gents started fighting each other. They were quickly pulled apart by some nearby gypsy boys, who for good measure gave them a good slapping and threw their expensive hats into the nearby bonfire. The gents were very angry but soon realised that taking on the boys would only end badly for them. Certainly the gypsy lads pulled no punches and at the slightest whiff of trouble gave the culprits a good beating. I also noted they were not averse to pulling out razor blades and threatening the wrongdoers in no uncertain terms.

Finally after nine o'clock the official prize fights ended. The gypsies' main man, Medlock Lee, came up to the ring and in a strong voice announced that the fighting was over and everyone should go home. This was underlined by dowsing the lanterns and bonfires. The city crowd got the message and started making their way back to the halt. There was a general feeling that everyone had got more than they bargained for. Clearly some had lost all their money, others had got beatings, perhaps from silly fights, or getting too fresh with the mollies. Even the lads who had sampled the mollies' delights seemed less than happy.

Then another thing occurred I did not expect. The punter who had stood beside us came over and whispered into my ear. "Word is that Billy has died. Keep it to yourself. We had best get out of here because there will be trouble over this, you mark my words."

The word seemed to have got around like wildfire and the city gents were all making their way back to the railway halt.

Virtually everyone had drunk too much and some were puking as well as pissing in the woods on the way back to the station.

The train came in on time and it was with a sense of relief that we left Low Street and headed back towards London.

NINETEEN

13th September, 1879

IT WAS THE NEXT DAY after our night out at Low Street that I met Bill again, this time at the Cheshire Cheese. I had been restless and sleeping badly. My mind was full of thoughts of what I should have done, and what I could do now.

I had Romero in my sights at the fight but had not challenged him in any way. Perhaps I was shocked by him being there, or the death of the boxer had left me confused. Whatever the reason I was not feeling good about myself, or life. Elisa was being held captive, being subjected to God knows what, and all I could do was to go drinking with Bill.

As per usual he was in good form, seemingly untouched by Low Street, though I, if truth be told, still had a queasy tummy; probably bad beer. After the usual banter I opened up to him.

"I just do not understand why I had Romero right there in front of me, and did nothing. I know we would have been hopelessly outnumbered but it feels like a missed opportunity. Scrivener as well, I should have pulled him to one side and quizzed him."

Bill looked at me in a fatherly way.

"What's done is done. It is how we progress things from here that counts now."

I searched for something positive.

"Well the event still gave us no clue as to where Romero is staying. I doubt that it's with the gypsies. I suspect he was just there bankrolling the fights. He could be anywhere."

Bill nodded. I continued.

"The chances are that he is based somewhere in Essex or London and I suspect Elisa will be nearby as well. This Scrivener guy clearly works in that part of Essex, so that limits the search area."

Bill was thinking, I could tell this by the odd look in his eyes. Finally he spoke.

"Perhaps Scrivener is the key to finding her? One thing you could do is write to him offering a photography job. When he turns up, grill him."

"It has already been done. I've written to him saying that Aunt Matilda in Horndon is bedbound so she needs a travelling photographer to take some pictures of her and the family. Once he is in the house we will squeeze him for information. Threaten him with the police. Anything to get him to talk.

"If he turns up at the shop the manager will pass on the letter I've written. I can only hope he takes the bait."

I ordered another pint and the session went on. Just as I had made up my mind to leave, Bill dropped in another nugget.

"I don't know if this has any relevance but I was looking at the shipping lists this morning. I noticed that the *River*

Plate is bound for Antwerp in Belgium. No clue as to why it should be going there."

I thought about this for a moment.

"The *River Plate* usually comes into the pool of London; I wonder why it's using Antwerp now?"

After some further conversation we ended our session and made our way back to our respective homes. I knew in my guts we should be doing more, but could not fathom what that should be.

TWENTY

Itchy Feet at the Weaver Arms, 23rd September

HENRY FRANKLAND WAS IN A foul mood again. He was now hanging around the bar of the Weaver Arms getting under Mary's feet.

Finally she had enough.

"What is the matter with you? You have been in a mood since you got back from Liverpool last month."

Frankland huffed.

"This is business. Man's work. You don't need to get involved."

"It's that Romero isn't it? He's left you holding the baby while he runs off with all the money."

He ground his teeth.

"There is nothing to worry about. I just need to have a clearer idea of what is going on. That is all."

She looked at him with disdain.

"The truth is that Romero has done a moonlight flit by all accounts. Left Liverpool and nobody knows where he is."

Frankland was not happy.

"Keep your nose out of business."

"It's true though isn't it? That's why you are in a mood. He has pissed off without giving you a passing thought."

He scowled then poured himself a drink of bitter from the tap into his tankard and without letting the head settle, threw it back.

She sniffed loudly.

"That won't sort things out."

The awkward silence that then ensued was broken by the Royal Mail telegram boy who came into the bar. The missive was addressed to Frankland. He read it intently.

"What is it?" she asked.

"It's from your sister Nettie, saying that I must come down to the Lovat immediately. That Mister Romero has left an envelope with a lot of cash inside it for me."

Mary scoffed and took the paper.

"It ain't from her. She don't write that well. And, if there was a load of cash in an envelope sitting around, she would have nicked it herself by now."

"Well that is as may be. It could be Romero himself telling her what to write. Whatever, I had best make tracks back to London. The sooner I get to the bottom of this, and get some cash in my back pocket, the better."

TWENTY-ONE

Lovat Arms, London, 24th September, Afternoon

THE NEXT DAY FRANKLAND MADE the rail journey back to the capital and by early afternoon had arrived at the Lovat Arms near Billingsgate. This was going to be awkward – some regulars might still remember him, so he pulled his collar up his face covering much of his port-wine stain and moved to the quietest corner of the bar. He didn't have to wait long. Nettie saw him immediately and gestured for him to come behind the bar and upstairs to the backroom. He did so. In the first-floor room were Romero and another swarthy looking man he did not immediately recognise.

Romero looked like his old self.

"Henry, so good to see you again. Let me introduce Pedro, Pedro Diaz, an old friend of mine. You might have come across him doing night watchman's duties at Thames Haven."

Frankland shook the outstretched hands. He took an immediate dislike to Pedro for no apparent reason. Romero continued.

"Good journey Henry?"

"No problems at all. Glad to see you, I was at a bit of a loss after you left Liverpool in such a hurry."

Romero smiled broadly showing some gold fillings to his back teeth.

"All history now. Things to be done. Exciting opportunities. Now I'll give you a look at my plans."

They sat down at a table and Romero brought out a map of the Thames estuary area. Then he spent the next thirty minutes running through a scheme to steal munitions and take them by barge to rendezvous with the *River Plate* in the estuary. It was a daring plan.

Frankland took it all in. It was a tall order but what options did he have? A chance of making his fortune working alongside Romero, or going back to Frodsham to tell Mary he was almost penniless. Finally Romero spoke.

"So are you alright with the plan, Henry?"

Frankland nodded. He wondered why Pedro was still standing in the room. Romero was pleased.

"Good. Full speed ahead on that then." There was a pause while he took in the atmosphere of the room. "One other little bit of business, and I would be grateful if you could work with Pedro on this."

He looked at Frankland, who reluctantly nodded.

"We had a bit of a problem at the prize fight at a gypsy camp. The local favourite, Jed Bibby, died from injuries in the ring. No great problem there but his wife then kicked off and told the Gravesend police that I am the guilty partner in all of this. That is not good, not good at all. I don't like my name being dragged through the mud. So she needs to be a taught a lesson. Pedro here has been sniffing around and found out that she has left her gypsy tribe altogether and just started working as a fortune teller at Rosherville Gardens in Gravesend. Good work, Pedro."

Pedro smiled which showed off his mess of missing teeth. It was not a pretty sight.

"So I was hoping you men might go to the gardens and basically… tell the woman her fortune. You understand me? Good. Pedro has a covered wagon and some chloroform. Get her into that and scare her to death. Make sure she keeps her mouth buttoned from now on. We understand each other? Good. So be on your way. Pedro will take you down to Gravesend. The sooner we can get this woman off our backs the sooner we can concentrate on the real business. Making some serious money. Am I not right Pedro?"

He smiled again. What an ugly oaf he was thought Frankland.

They left by the back entrance. Nearby a horse stood patiently waiting with a covered wagon behind it. Without further ado they climbed onto the box seat and set off on the long drive to Gravesend.

They said very little. Frankland disliked the man and he got the impression that the feeling was mutual. The journey was tiresome and they didn't arrive in Gravesend until well into the evening, so they had little option but to sleep in the back of the wagon. It was best that nobody knew they were in the town.

TWENTY-TWO

Rosherville Gardens, 25th September

IT WAS A TIRESOME NIGHT, two men in a space little more than six feet by four on top of straw bedding. Frankland noticed that Pedro was smelly. Probably didn't wash very often. His animal smell probably appealed to those awful Latin women. With this unkind thought he finally drifted off to sleep.

The next day dawned and it was a fine one. Plenty of sunshine to draw people to the pleasure gardens. They had now worked out the details of the plan. Frankland was to be a recently widowed gentleman trying to make contact with his dead wife through the auspices of the gypsy woman, Rose. Pedro would play the part of a Catholic priest and help Rose out of the gardens and over to the wagon. The pretext would be that Rose had a relative dying in hospital and the priest was bringing her the bad news. In fact Rose would only be walking with them because she had a gun pointed at her back. Then they would get her into the wagon and apply the chloroform.

They spent the morning wandering the backstreets keeping a low profile but finding a café to eat in. It was a working man's place so their rough appearance would not raise any eyebrows. Frankland went to the lavatory and tried to make himself look presentable. He had decided to change into his old military uniform – soldiers coming back from their duties in the empire were a common sight and it gave him some credibility and gravitas. Finding a Catholic priest's gown was not so easy but eventually one was found at a second-hand clothes shop. It was far from perfect but would be adequate for the day.

After midday the pleasure gardens were opened and they could see amongst the entertainments that there was a tent with the sign alongside – Madame Gypsy Lee – fortune teller and spiritualist. Pedro nodded. This was their quarry.

They paid the sixpence entrance fees, walked in and noted the fine landscaping of the place, which was set in an overgrown disused quarry which had now changed into something akin to a pleasant green valley with an entrance at its north end, close to a pier from which visitors by the river from London could disembark. Although infamous for its mollies and pickpockets, it was still an inviting and pleasant enough place to spend the day with any boredom alleviated by the entertainments. In the grounds were sellers of everything under the sun. Watercress and seafood stalls abounded and all the various fairground-type amusement – which would quickly empty your pockets. At the end of the fairground area was a single gypsy tent and a sign outside advertising 'Madame Lee – World famous fortune teller'.

Now getting into the tent would be easy, anyone with money could achieve that. It was getting her out and all the way through the gardens to the cart outside, that was the challenge. The plan was that whilst Frankland was in the tent having his fortune told, Pedro would be getting changed in the latrines, into the plain brown priest's robe, topped with white collar. He would arrive at the gypsy tent a few minutes after, and provide a suitably austere and solemn escort to get Rose out of the pleasure gardens.

Dressed in his uniform, Frankland walked up to the tent. The gypsy woman, whose nom de plume was Madame Lee but he knew as Rose Bibby, sat outside knitting but had soon caught his eye.

"You look like a man burdened with troubles, let me read your fortune, and with luck, you'll have some good news about the future."

He did not want to appear too keen.

"I do not think so, madam. My wife passed away recently and I have only come to the gardens for some relaxation."

"All the more reason for having your fortune told. I am the best. And it will only cost you a half crown."

His face broke into a cautious smile and he had soon deposited the money in her hand. She opened the tent flap, and ushered him inside and then followed.

Inside the tent it was fairly claustrophobic.

Rose had a crystal ball on a low table in the centre, and they sat either side of it on foldable timber chairs. She stared at the ball, and then turned to him. "So would you like to just talk, or shall we go straight into the fortune telling?"

Henry had no time to waste. He reached into his jacket pocket and pulled out a small revolver.

"I am afraid, Madame Lee, or is it Mrs Bibby…" Suddenly the atmosphere in the tent chilled. "… That I have come here on more serious business. I have a friend who needs to talk to you in private. Just a conversation that's all. Nothing to worry about. If you can leave the tent without fuss and walk over to the south entrance alongside the priest who is standing outside. Do so without fuss, and without drawing attention to yourself. If anyone asks what is happening just cry and we will do the talking. I will be alongside you with the gun aimed at your heart should you try to escape, or raise the alarm in any way. Is that clear?"

She was now worried.

"Yes."

"On your way then, but slowly."

She left the tent and immediately came upon Pedro standing alongside it dressed in a full Catholic priest's outfit.

"Come now, my child."

He gently put his hand on her shoulder. Frankland turned the sign advertising the fortune telling around, and then stood on the other side of her.

They solemnly started walking towards the entrance. After a few paces another stallholder, a gentleman dressed in a full pearly king outfit, came over to see what was happening. Henry was straight on the case.

"I am afraid that Madame Lee has suffered an unexpected bereavement. We are taking her to the hospital now and will give her as much comfort as we are able."

Without a word the pearly king doffed his flat cap and stood with it tight to his trouser waistband.

"God bless you, madam," he said, then dipped his head to stare at the ground.

After that, the walk passed without fuss although Frankland was constantly on edge in case she tried to run off. Thankfully she did not. Pedro seemed to have no problem playing the priest, and thankfully she kept quiet. The contrivance worked well and they were let out of the gardens without a murmur from the gatemen, who were clearly taken in by this and even opened the gate for their convenience.

They were soon standing behind Pedro's covered wagon in the side street. She was now getting concerned.

"What do you want? Did Romero send you?"

Frankland kept his cool. This was all in a day's work.

"Get into the wagon and we can talk."

She reluctantly obeyed and clambered up into the wagon, skilfully manoeuvring through the canvas flap entrance. Pedro then followed her in whilst Frankland went to the box seat to take charge of the carriage.

As soon as he was able Pedro grabbed her around the neck, and pushed a handkerchief loaded with chloroform over her mouth. She gave out muffled cries for help but within a minute these had died off. She was now fully sedated.

Frankland looked around. The street was quiet. So far. So good. He shouted to Pedro.

"Shall I head to the ferry?"

From inside the covered cart he responded.

"Yes, she's down now. Over the ferry, to the north bank. To the safe house. Don't worry, nobody will check what we have in the wagon when going across."

They were soon at the town quay. The ferry was busy and nobody had any interest of what was inside the wagon.

In just five minutes they had crossed the river. Frankland manoeuvred the horse and wagon away from the ferry stage in the direction of Fort Road. At this point the horse became frisky and agitated. Frankland stepped down from the box seat and calmed the horse by gently patting it. He was aware at that moment of a noise from inside the wagon. Perhaps Rose had awoken early?

"What's going on?" He shouted.

Pedro shouted back, "It's nothing, just carry on to the farm. I'll tell you then."

Whatever, Pedro could easily handle her. He got back onto the box seat, took the reins and gently encouraged the horse up Fort Road. It was still a very warm day and perhaps the horse was sweating because of it. They were slowly trotting along Fort Road towards Marsh Farm. They were the only vehicle on this quiet road that crossed the marshlands.

In a few minutes they were at the farm and had pulled up around the back, on the marshes side, where few prying eyes could see. Frankland calmed the horse, jumped off and went to the wagon. He was not prepared for the sight that greeted him.

Pedro was wiping blood from a massive knife. He looked guilty. Beneath him the gypsy woman had clearly had her neck cut open and was dead. There were copious amounts of blood everywhere.

Frankland shouted, "What the hell have you done?"
Pedro squirmed. "She came round, and then started kicking and screaming, fighting me. I told her to keep quiet and threatened her with my knife on her throat, but then the wagon bumped over something, the knife slipped, and her throat got cut."

Frankland was furious but the deed was done. They dragged her body off the cart and took it into a disused room in the farm. Henry knew this was not an answer but he needed time to think. It didn't take him too long. This kidnap was Pedro's doing and so was her death. He had his own work to do, organising the munitions theft.

"I am going down to Tilbury station to telegram Romero about this, and then get back to my real work. You can sort out a safe space to dispose of the body. It's your problem. It's certainly not my business anymore. If someone finds her, you get done for murder. Do I make myself clear?"

"You can't just do that to me. We were both in it together."

"I never wanted to work with you. You sweaty, gaucho bastard. I only did it because Romero told me to. Get it sorted. I never want to see your ugly face again."

At that Frankland tidied himself up, making sure he had no visible bloodstains, and walked the half mile to the station cursing to himself all the way.

From inside Marsh Farm, Elisa had heard the noise of the cart approaching and then men arguing with each other. She recognised one of the voices as her gaoler, Pedro. It made her sick to her stomach to realise she once had been his lover. He was rough even then. She often thought back to the first time with him. She was much younger, more naïve. Did he rape her? He was certainly very assertive but she thought that all men were like that and it was her role to succumb to everything he wanted. Now the thought of those long ago days in the Argentine made her feel physically sick.

The argument outside ended and soon Pedro appeared at the doorway. He looked at her, checked her chains, scowled at the chamber pot then took some hard biscuits, stale bread, and cheese from the cupboard and left it by her side. She stared at him.

"What is going on? I could hear you arguing."

He looked at her with disdain.

"None of your business."

She did not like this.

"When did you become such an animal? You were never this bad in the old days, you cared for me then."

He scoffed. "You were always just meat to me. Easy meat. You are lucky that Romero still has regard for you or else you would be getting more than bread and water from me."

She spat. "You pig."

He walked out of the room without looking back.

She sat listening intently. He was in the next room moving something about for a while. Then silence, so he had probably left.

She looked around again. The room was undecorated, or had not been decorated in years. It had a door, a larder-type cupboard alongside in which food was kept, and a straw bed on which she slept. The bare floor had simply a plate for her food, a mug for water and a chamber pot. She was chained to the wall but the chain was long enough that she could manoeuvre into the bed of straw or sit and stand on the chamber pot. Also there was a window above the straw bed, or rather what had been a window but was now boarded up. Oddly though, the curtain rail, which looked like it was forged from wrought iron, was still in place but the curtains had been taken down. She reached up and felt the end of the curtain pole. It was affixed into the wall by some nuts and bolts but it looked like a makeshift job. She pulled at it, and then pulled again. Eventually one end gave, then the other. She had the curtain pole in her hands.

She walked over to the door stretching the chains to their limit; to her surprise she found Pedro had not even locked the door. She stretched and could just see into the other room – presumably it had been some kind of storage room for boots and tools, probably for men working on the land to get clean before coming into the parlour, which was presumably the room she was in. But the biggest shock was what was laid flat in the room – close to the door she was looking through. It was the body of a woman. She could see her face, a gypsy woman's face, now pasty white with strands of her curly black hair hanging limply. She was obviously dead.

Elisa knew she had to find out more. She used the curtain pole's jagged end to find some purchase on the woman's clothing. The woman was a mess, obviously killed by a knife to the throat, she had bled profusely and this blood was congealed over her clothing. She tugged away. At first she thought it was hopeless then the body moved towards her an inch or two. Then a good few inches, then a foot. Finally she could stretch far enough to pull at the clothing and drag the corpse towards her. She was now almost exhausted but carried on. She did not recognise the woman at all. What was she doing here? Why had Pedro or one of his gang killed her? It was all just so awful. Then some sixth sense made her do an odd thing. She bent over and smelt the woman's midriff area, then a bit below, and then pushed her nose down even closer. It was only slight but definite. She could smell a man's semen. No doubt. She recoiled. So not only had she been murdered but probably raped as well. Before, or after death? The thought made her physically retch. How had Pedro sunk so low? This man was filth. Almost as if he was reading her mind, Pedro suddenly opened the outside door and came in. He dragged the corpse away then set about Elisa, pushing her back to the straw bed, wrenching the curtain rail out of her hands. He said nothing, just stared like a wild animal. She was scared but unbowed.

"How could you be such an animal? You're filth. Filth!"

"Shut up, woman. If I wasn't told to keep you alive I would do exactly the same to you. Get back on your bed."

At that he stormed out of the room with the curtain pole. This time making sure he locked the door from the outside.

She lay back on the straw matting. Things were going from bad to worse. Somehow she was now in a hell with no obvious chance of escape. She sobbed.

TWENTY-THREE

London, 24th September

A FULL TEN DAYS OR so after my meeting with Bill in the Cheshire Cheese, I went to see Sullivan at the yard. I had wanted to see him earlier but I had been struck down by a stomach bug. Probably caught at the night of the prize fights, so I had spent the last week in a pit of sickness and depression. Luckily Sullivan seemed in a better mood. He was leaning back in his chair and lighting up a cigarette – the new kind of smoking, popular with the young men – he put the cigarette down and looked at me.

"Something interesting has turned up, not that far from the marshes where the Hope boy perished. A prize fighter died, we believe in an illegal fight near Low Street, his wife is also now missing. Rumour has it that a Spaniard called Romero was somehow involved, possibly the promoter of the bout."

He sat back smugly. I jumped in. "I know, I was there. At Low Street, with Bill, watching the fights."

Sullivan immediately jumped out of his chair, clearly annoyed.

"Why did you not tell me about this?"

I answered honestly. "We were obviously there incognito, pretended we were rich city gents out for a flutter on the fights. I heard the boxer had died but had no proof. And Romero being there was a total shock to us. Trouble was when you're surrounded by dozens of drunken gypsies, all tooled up, what do you do? I did think about informing you the next day but Romero would have been far away by then. He wouldn't have been part of the gypsy camp, just using their facilities for the fights. He could be anywhere."

Sullivan settled down and looked me in the eye.

"Quite. And the gypsy woman. Any clues as to her whereabouts?"

"Nothing. She was clearly very angry with Romero. Probably blaming him for her husband's death. I assumed that once things had calmed down and everyone had sobered up things would just revert to normal; the gypsies would go on their way. The boxer's death would be hushed up and nobody would be any the wiser."

Sullivan fiddled with some papers in front of him almost as if unsure as to whether he should be sharing information.

"That is the usual case with the Romany community, but oddly, last week, the woman turned up at Gravesend police station and told the desk sergeant the full story – her husband Jed Bibby's death, and how it was all Romero's fault. Then no sooner had she arrived, than she disappeared. That was the last anyone saw of her. The local police traced the group of gypsies; they had just crossed on the Tilbury ferry to go over to a farm in Kent for the hop picking, but nobody would say anything. Half of them pretended they couldn't understand English. The woman was not with them, the prize fights never happened. You get the picture."

We sat looking at each other for a few moments. I broke the ice.

"So why did you not tell me this sooner?"

"Pressure of work, old boy. Dead gypsies not a police priority."

I was furious but spoke calmly. "So what should we do now?" Sullivan had a slight smugness to his smile as he looked me in the eye.

"It just so happens that we have had some good luck. I believe you dropped off a letter with the manager at the photography shop in Chancery Lane asking for Scrivener to contact you if he came in for supplies."

"Yes."

"Well you are in luck. Scrivener has written back, saying he is available and even giving the address of his workplace. It appears that he is based at Goldsmiths Wharf in Argent Street, Grays, near the river. Probably keeps his horse and wagon stabled there as well."

He had a satisfied smile, and then continued.

"Of course at this stage there is not much we can do about it. There is no evidence of his direct involvement, so an arrest or a warrant to search his premises would not be possible at this time, I'm afraid."

My erstwhile elation turned to anxiety.

"So the evidence I have provided is not sufficient for you to do anything?"

"I am afraid not. At best these are just theories of a possible involvement in aiding and abetting the kidnap of this young lady, Miss Pound."

"But what about the link between the photographs taken of Elisa and this man?"

Sullivan sighed. "All a bit circumstantial I'm afraid. You see forensics is a new beast. The judge and jury are not really aware of their importance yet. I might swear that the pictures are on the kind of paper purchased by Scrivener, but that may not be enough. In any case he may well have been commissioned to take the pictures in complete ignorance of the fact that Miss Pound was being held against her will."

Another awkward silence. Finally Sullivan spoke. "So what do you intend to do now?"

"I appreciate what you've told me, though it leaves a nasty taste in the mouth. I think my first move will be to talk to Edward Hope's sister Matilda. She lives in Horndon on the hill. She must have seen Scrivener's horse and wagon in her area, perhaps she might have some idea where Elisa is held."

Sullivan nodded. We shook hands and I left. There was much to be done.

I immediately telegraphed Matilda to let her know I needed to see her. She responded quickly that afternoon, so the next morning I set out for Horndon, via a train to Stanford and hansom cab. I arrived at Matilda's house.

TWENTY-FOUR

Matilda's House, Horndon, 25th September

MATILDA CAME TO THE DOOR and greeted me with a cautious smile. I wondered how much time she spent alone in this big house. She always wore similar black outfits and was probably quite lonely, so pleased to have visitors.

For the next half hour I tried as best I could to fill her in on the progress so far. I realised I was failing because instead of making progress on finding the killer of Fontaine, I was now embroiled in seeking to rescue Elisa. I asked her about Scrivener, and yes, she had seen his horse and wagon but thought nothing of it. I pushed her on the subject of properties in the area where just possibly the young lady might be incarcerated. Still no progress – just endless cups of tea from the large pot and a good selection of shortbread biscuits. This was going nowhere.

Then the penny dropped. Matilda stood up and went over to a bureau on the side of the parlour and unlocked the drawers.

"I have just remembered, so long ago, it slipped my mind. Edward sold a number of properties to Mister Romero about the same time that he bought the land on Stanford marshes. I am surprised he did not mention it to you."

At that she brought out reams of paper. Maps, title deeds, list of addresses. I stood over the bureau going through these meticulously while Matilda resumed her ritual of tea pouring and sugar stirring.

The documents were often unduly confusing due to the legalese-type descriptions but I could see a number of potential properties worth investigating. Of course Romero may well have sold them on, but it was worth checking. Two that caught my eye were Oozedam Farm at Fobbing, and Marsh Farm at Tilbury. A lot of the other deeds were for parcels of farmland defined by hand-coloured maps which did not have a house on them. It took almost an hour to copy all the information down. Even Matilda was getting to the dregs of the teapot now. I turned to her. "I have one more favour to ask."

"Ask away."

"Do you know anybody that is handy with tools? Able to work under pressure."

She looked perplexed.

"In short I need someone to help me break into premises at night. Not to steal anything, just to find some documents that might be of use in finding Miss Pound."

Matilda thought for a while then came up with an answer.

"You might find the local blacksmith's boy useful. James his name is. He'll be across the road working the forge with his father."

I thanked her profusely and set off for the blacksmith's forge.

It was only a hundred yards from Matilda's to the forge. I could see the name 'Baldwin's farrier and ironsmiths' above a half height entrance. From inside I could feel the heat of the forge radiating out through the barn-style hatch doorway into the street. A stout gentleman, middle aged with a mop of grey hair, ruddy face and wearing a well-used leather apron, caught my eyes. He put down the irons he was hammering at tong's length and came over to me.

"Can I help you sir?"

He put out a gnarled, weather-beaten hand and grasped mine. It was the firmest handshake I had ever had. The man had an iron grip which he was probably not even aware of.

"Hello, I am sorry to disturb you but my name is William Reeves. I am a private detective working for Edward Hope, investigating the death of his grandson Fontaine."

The mention of Hope clearly meant much to him.

"Edward Hope, a fine man, I often speak to his sister Matilda, charming lady. Poor Fontaine, lovely boy. If I can do anything to help."

"The truth is, Mister Baldwin…"

"Call me Theo."

"Well, Theo, I am requiring a very big favour indeed. I need a job doing tonight and after talking to Matilda, I am of the impression that your boy, James, might be perfect for it."

Theo bellowed out, "Jamie over here."

A lad appeared, probably in his teens, a very thin and

wiry looking individual with pointed nose, inquisitive eyes – a bit ferret-like in his demeanour.

"This gentleman, Mister Reeves, has a job in mind that he thinks you could help with."

Jamie smiled. "What is it, sir?"

I stumbled over my words a little, this was a big ask.

"The truth is I need some documents that are held inside a shed. Down in Grays, by the waterfront. I will not be damaging the property or stealing anything, just getting in and out."

There was an awkward silence that I filled.

"I am investigating Fontaine Hope's death and finding these papers is crucial to me finding his killers."

Theo looked at his son.

"That is fine then, sir. If it helps get the killers James would be only too happy to help."

"And I would pay you for your troubles of course."

"Do you hear that, boy? You are even getting paid for something you'll enjoy doing."

Theo turned to me. "No problem, sir. What needs to be done?"

"I am just stopping over with Matilda at the moment. If I can come back here just before sunset, say six thirty. Have you a horse and cart we can use to get to Grays?"

Theo answered without hesitation. "No problem at all, sir, and I'll make sure James has all the gear needed for some gentle breaking in. Being a locksmith is one of our sidelines anyway. Surprising the number of people who lock themselves out of their own homes."

At that we shook hands. I knew I had chosen right. If James couldn't find a way into Scrivener's shed, then nobody could.

After a late tea with Matilda – I think she was enjoying the company – I departed at the allotted time. James and Theo were ready and waiting. Luckily it was Jamie's horse, so he would take the reins. Theo waved us off. The sun was setting now so we kept up a good pace, mostly along the London Road towards Grays. An hour later we stopped outside the Theobald Arms in Argent Street, a stone's throw from the river Thames. This part of the world was popular with seamen. In fact the barges would be moored on the river in front of the pub so that the bargees could keep an eye on them while drinking. The problem though was that with so many inns along the street, which ran up from the Theobald Arms into the town, there were too many people about. There was no other option than to pull into a quiet corner and wait. By nine o'clock we had had enough. Or Jamie had at least. He was clearly a young man who would like to see some action, and sitting waiting brought on a bout of fidgeting in him which did little to calm my senses. It was time for action.

The shed used by Scrivener was at an address near the corner of Argent Street and the high street, just behind the White Hart public house, down a narrow lane which had probably once been used by the night soil men. Luckily the shed had a small sign on it advertising 'Scrivener's Photography' so we knew we were in the right place.

James decided the horse and cart would be safest left outside the White Hart so anyone would assume we were drinkers and not up to anything untoward.

We stepped down from the box seat, quietened the horses, and then softly walked down the wide alley towards the shed. There was no sign of guard dogs, and no sound or smell of stabled horses.

On reaching the shed we weighed up the options for opening the heavy timber door, which was about seven foot square and covered most of the alleyway frontage. Within seconds Jimmy had got the suitable tools out of his bag. I nodded and within seconds he was soon gently prising the woodwork with his jemmy, or should I say, range of jemmies and chisels; he seemed to have brought the entire contents of his father's workshop. Finally, and with a gentle crack, the doors opened.

Inside the shed it was pitch black and we could only see the outline of Scrivener's wagon. Jamie had brought a small kerosene lantern with him which he lit with great care. We looked around but there was precious little to see, just the wagon and a stout iron cabinet alongside it, abutting the side of the shed. I gestured for James to unlock it. We had soon learned how to communicate without speaking. This time he went for the lock with what appeared to be a long and well-used skeleton key. Working by the lamplight he fiddled with this for some time. Just as I thought we would need a new plan, the cabinet doors opened. He smiled. We were in.

I knew what I was looking for. On the top shelf was a heavy ledger, I hauled it out and resting it on the top of the cabinet, scoured the page, whilst Jamie held the lamp above our heads. The answers soon came. The page contained a list of his clients, the date of the work, the price and the addresses of the locations he had to visit. Immediately I saw the name Romero and alongside it the location – MF, Tilbury and various dates and times. From what I had seen earlier in Matilda's, I surmised that MF must be Marsh Farm – a property bought by Romero many years back from

Hope. The dates were also important; they matched with dates on the newspaper shown in the photograph of Elisa. There was no doubt now. Scrivener was the photographer and Romero the client. That was all I needed.

We quickly replaced the ledger back to its original location and closed the cabinet. The main timber door might be a bigger problem but James was already on the case, he was gently gluing the splintered wood back together, and repairing the hasp and bracket to the outside. The glue smelt of cooked animal bones but perhaps this might wear off by the next day. Obviously it was a bodged job, but with luck, and hoping that Scrivener opened and closed the doors without looking too closely in the morning, we might just get away with it.

We returned to the cart, stepped up on to the box seat, gently stirred the horses into life and made our way out of Grays and back to Horndon. It had been a tiring night, but successful.

We had achieved our aim in total, now it was just a case of getting safely back to Horndon and awaiting the telegraph office opening in the morning, from where I could contact Sullivan, and beg him to raid Marsh Farm. I had a gut feeling that we needed to do this soon. Time was not on our side. If we could get to the farm, then with luck, we could rescue poor Elisa.

TWENTY-FIVE

The Marshlands, 26th September

I slept badly, in fact hardly at all. Elisa was playing on my mind. I had this bad feeling that time was of the essence and I had to move quickly. Luckily breakfast was taken early and I was out in time to be first in the queue at the post office to send the telegraph off. I knew that logically I should return home and await Sullivan's response but I was too upset and anxious. I walked around to Baldwin's and thanked Theo and Jamie for all their help. Then I managed to acquire their delivery wagon for the day. Although I paid him, I think that Mr Baldwin's generosity was exemplary and perhaps tied in to his respect for the Hope family. Despite this goodwill it was late morning before the blacksmith's rounds were finished and I got the reins of the pair.

Collecting my gear from Matilda's I set off for Tilbury. I just had to get a sneaky look at Marsh Farm. It took me just over the hour later before I took the road downhill from West

Tilbury onto the flat marshlands that led towards Tilbury Fort. Luckily Fort Road was an ancient thoroughfare, and well used – it being the only road that picked its way through the marshlands to the river. So it was perfectly good enough for my wagon. Ahead of me now was the railway crossing on Fort Road, which I knew from the map was less than a mile from the farm. I could see immediately an issue. South of the railway running down to the Thames was about a mile of flat featureless marsh with just three visible buildings: Marsh Farm itself, Tilbury Fort beyond it, and Riverside station to the west. There was nothing else. Anyone going to Marsh Farm would be highly visible. Luckily alongside the railway was a short thoroughfare, boasting the name Bryanston Road. It was a short street with just a handful of cottages along it, which I assume were probably for employees of the railway company. I decided to park up the pair there, and set off on foot. I chose to walk in a south-easterly direction instead of taking the direct route to the farm, which would have been due south along Fort Road. My chosen route would take me to the back, the open marshlands side of the farm. I crossed the railway line then tried to pick out a safe route through the marshes.

The ground conditions were terrible, just marsh and saltings – one false move and I would be up to my neck in brackish water and mud. I was wearing my green tweed jacket, so hopefully, if spotted, I might be mistaken for a wildfowler looking to shoot ducks. I moved slowly, often doubling back to find a route through the awkward swirls, my head low.

I knew from the maps I had seen at Matilda's that Marsh Farm had its own quay to its south-west aspect bounding onto a wide body of water which boasted the name: Ordnance Creek. I could only assume from that that at some time in the past munitions had been brought to the fort via this strange waterway that wrapped itself around the fort's outer boundary – perhaps unloading ammunition this way avoided the uncertainties of trying to perform this task on the tidal Thames at the front of the fort.

As I moved to the east I could now see beyond the farmhouse a Thames barge moored at the quay. I ducked down then reached for my opera glasses. I could soon see activity taking place; something was being loaded onto the barge from the back of a cart. I waited patiently. Loading complete, the now empty cart moved off down the short track towards Fort Road. Then to my surprise it turned hard left and seemed to be making its way across the timber bridges that span the outer moats of the fort. In a couple of minutes it had reached the landward gate at the rear of the fort – its frontage faced the river to the south. The gate opened and the cart disappeared into the fort. So what was all this then? The penny dropped. They were taking munitions from the fort to the barge. Was this all official, or did Frankland and Romero have a hand in this undertaking?

I wanted to get a better view but now seemed to be stuck on an island behind a substantial fleet of water of indeterminate depth, which blocked my progress south or east. This was frustrating as I could only see half of what was occurring, as the farm building was blocking much of my view of the barge loading area. I was stuck in that location for almost an hour more. I could catch glimpses of a horse and cart going backwards and forwards to the land gate of the fort but not what was being loaded on the barge. I looked at my pocket watch, almost one o'clock; I had memorised the river water heights and guessed we were now close to high tide. As if on cue the ropes were thrown on board the barge, which had now stretched out its spritsail to catch the wind. It gently moved away from the quay, taking a course towards the opening of the waterway onto the river. I watched it sail majestically down Ordnance Creek, which was perhaps three furlongs in length. Although common workhorses of the river, the height and spread of the blood red sails on these spritsail barges never lost their power to impress when the wind carried them at speed. I tried to get every detail of the barge. It was called *The Rising Sun*, the lettering proudly emblazoned near its prow. It was typical of the barges that worked the river, though I noted it had no red marking or flag, which was the requirement for barges transporting explosives. I could see the two-man crew working hard to set the sails and make quick and safe progress. If there were other people on board, they would have to be in the hold.

Within ten minutes the barge had manoeuvred out from the creek and into the river, heading due east, presumably towards the estuary. The heavy timber entrance doors to the fort's land gate were now closed and there was no sign of activity. The farm was also dead quiet. I would dearly have loved to have got up close to the farmhouse and peeked through its windows but the topography was totally against me. These saltings were lethal, one false step and at best I would get a boot full of mud, at worst I could be stuck in something akin to quicksand. I decided that I had seen enough today and gingerly made my way back through the high sedge and marshy ground to the railway crossing.

Nobody seemed to be about in Bryanston Road so I remounted the box seat of the cart and roused the horses back to life. One part of me wanted to go to the fort itself and confront the people inside but I had to know my limitations. I was not the police and trying to browbeat the military personnel on site might not go down well. So I set off back to Horndon.

TWENTY-SIX

Marsh Farm, 26th September

LITTLE DID I KNOW THAT events had already proceeded, right in front of my eyes, in plain sight.

Earlier that morning, probably around six o'clock, Elisa had been woken from her fitful sleep by an agitated Pedro.

"Come on, get up. We are going on a journey."

At that he undid her chains. Within five minutes she was on her feet and being pulled by him through the door. Even in the half-light she could detect where she was, it was somewhere out on the marshes. The air was heavy and wet. He put his arm inside Elisa's and marched her to the front of the building. In front of her was a Thames barge lying at anchor, and in the distance, what looked like an old fort. It was the first fresh air she had tasted in many weeks but it did not last long. Within a few minutes she was on board the barge and taken below into the hull where another set of chains awaited her. So that was that. A brief taste of the outside world, now back as a prisoner on an old Thames barge with the ship's timbers already feeling hard, cold and unyielding against her posterior.

Not a lot happened for a while but later on that morning the hatch to the hold was opened and men she had never seen started loading up the hold with barrels of what, from the markings on the kegs, might well have been explosives. They gave her a cursory glance but were clearly under the cosh and had a lot of work to do in a short time. This loading went on all morning and the time must have now been close to noon, though there was no way of knowing for sure. She then heard another argument from outside the boat, it sounded like the two men who had been arguing before.

"Get the cart back to the fort and we're all done. I am staying on board getting the gear properly stacked." There was a sense of annoyance in his voice. Another man, this time with a Spanish accent, answered curtly.

 "Alright. How is it I get to do all the real graft?"

She recognised it as Pedro's voice.

"Because you're a lazy fucker. They don't know how to work in your part of the world."

At that the argument ended and within seconds the English-sounding gentleman appeared at the hatch to the hold.

"Sorry about the language, madam. My name is Frankland by the way, Henry Frankland. Try to get as comfortable as you can. We will sail once our Latin friend returns."

At that he left her and spent his time re-arranging the barrels and boxes.

Meanwhile, back inside Marsh Farm, Pedro had decided enough was enough.

"You men. Help me with this."

He gestured for them to go into the back room of the farm, and pointed to Rose's body.

"Get it onto the cart. We are taking it back to the fort."

The men looked perplexed but they were the type who never queried an order, just did it and took the money. Pedro then carted the corpse down the road then across the outer moat bridges back inside the fort. He had decided to have some fun, and at Frankland's expense.

Twenty minutes later he emerged and returned to the barge.

Frankland and the barge's captain, a man named Houghton, were impatient to see him but it was the old soldier doing all the talking.

"How long does it take to tidy things up? Let's get going!" he barked.

The loading was over, the voyage had started.

TWENTY-SEVEN

Scotland Yard,
26th September

TIME WAS NOW NOT ON my side. The trip back to Horndon took over an hour. Then I felt obliged to profusely thank the Baldwins, I had to also collect my gear from Matilda and make my way back to Stanford station. I decided to get the train to Fenchurch Street then change onto the new underground line to Westminster, arriving in late afternoon at Scotland Yard.

My luck was in, Sullivan was at his desk and I saw him immediately. I went through the information I had, and how I was almost certain that Elisa was being held at Marsh Farm, added to which there was a possibility that Romero was also using this as a base for secreting explosives out of Tilbury Fort. Sullivan listened intently then left me alone while he spoke to his colleagues. Ten minutes later he re-emerged.

"Very well. We will raid Marsh Farm first thing tomorrow."

My relief was palpable. We discussed details, or as much as he was willing to share with a non policeman. Finally it was decided that I could attend the raid as an observer. I was to get the first train in the morning to Tilbury Riverside station where he would meet me. It was now almost 5p.m. I bade him farewell and made tracks back to Whitechapel for a few hours' sleep before the big day.

It was early evening and already dark when I arrived at my own front door, five minutes' walk away from Whitechapel station. Standing by the door was a large man, for a moment I felt some concern, then realisation dawned, it was Bill Barrington! He smiled for a second then returned to his normal grumpy persona.

"Come on then. Let me in. It's freezing out here."

"Bill, are you alright? I thought you were staying at home till your ribs healed?"

Bill grunted. "Waste of time. I was bored stiff, needed to get back to the action. Now here I am, right as rain."

I warmly shook his hand and opened the front door. Within a few minutes I had the fire alight and Bill settled in my best armchair. I then spent the next hour going through all that had occurred and my hopes for tomorrow.

We were on our second cup of tea; I thought I had best keep the booze away from him. When I had finished recounting everything, Bill smiled at me and leaned in. He clearly had something to say.

"A pal of mine who works in Antwerp is over here on business. Tells me that the *River Plate* has been berthed up on the Scheldt in Antwerp for a good few days. Seems that after it left Liverpool it sailed down the Irish Sea as if going back to South America. Funny thing was that instead of going south, it turned east up the English Channel. Happily moored up at the best berth in Antwerp now."

He sat back looking pleased. I was genuinely surprised.

"What is it doing there? That's well out of its way."

Bill smiled. It was good to see him enjoying himself.

"It may have something to do with the Belgian king, Leopold. I don't know if you've been following the story but the king is dead keen to start a Belgian empire. Apparently he is jealous of what the British and French have got in Africa. So he has set up an organisation to survey the River Congo area. He even has Stanley, the explorer, working for him. You know, the American who found Livingstone. Of course it's not about surveying, or taking Christianity, or whatever, to Africa; it is about making that Congo region part of the Belgian Empire."

He sat back.

"So how does the *River Plate* get involved?"

"Simple really. Stanley has already been sent by ship from Antwerp to Boma, near the mouth of the Congo River. As I say, surveying is just a front for conquering the land and extracting materials. My guess is that Romero has been paid a pretty penny to stop off on his way back to the Argentine, with a load of something useful for achieving their ends."

"Explosives? Guns?" I ventured.

"Your guess is as good as mine, but if there is serious money to be made, Romero will have sniffed it out."

We both sat for a few seconds in the quiet.

"I saw a barge *The Rising Sun* leaving Marsh Farm with goods from Tilbury Fort. Might have been ordnance put on board. Perhaps that could be destined for Antwerp, then on to Boma?"

"Who knows?"

I stroked my chin.

"We need to be careful here. We could be adding two and two, and making five. Could you sniff around your contacts, see if you can find out anything else about the *River Plate*, maybe see if the barge has been spotted anywhere as well. Mind you, Antwerp is a fair run for a barge; seems unlikely."

"No problem. I'm not up to chasing thugs across the marshes anyway."

Bill had one more thing to add.

"The other thing is that the weather in the English Channel is bad at the moment. The winds will also be affecting the Thames estuary. Could be gales, so if the barge is trying to cross the Dover Straits, it could be in for a rough ride."

I sat for a moment in thought. This was all conjecture; we had no real idea where it would be headed. Also, I did not want to exhaust Bill. After some persuasion I hailed a hansom cab passing the house. I then ordered Bill to get himself home, and have a good sleep. He had done more than enough to help me.

TWENTY-EIGHT

27th September

THE NEXT DAY DAWNED AND after much scrabbling about I made the first train to Tilbury Riverside. I was met on board by Inspector Sullivan and his assistant who bore the interesting name of Thoroughgood. Our conversation was a little stilted, this was clearly too early for any of us. At Grays station four burly police constables came on board. So I realised that there were six police lined up for the raid with the only discernible weaponry some heavy black truncheons.

Sullivan's sidekick did carry a small but clearly heavy bag with him but what was contained within I had no idea. I could only pray that those at Marsh Farm were unarmed.

We arrived at Tilbury Riverside and Sullivan waited for the early morning workers going across to Gravesend on the ferry to depart. We were now pretty much on our own, with nothing between us and Marsh Farm but a half mile of marsh and the ancient track known as Fort Road, which passed north of the fort and led to the farm gates. One useful piece of information was that the station manager had his own telegraph connection and Sullivan had arranged for a direct link to Scotland Yard to speed up messaging.

We set off up the road; the constables were obviously conspicuous in their black uniforms and helmets. This was certainly no surprise raid, unless that is, everyone was still asleep. From my reading I had found out a little about the farm; it was purely the centre for livestock grazing, with its cattle spread far and wide over the marshlands. How it made a living from that I had no idea.

We walked on past the fort noting the land gate at the back of the fortification immediately to our right side, due south. Then to the east I could get a better sight of Ordnance Creek with its modest stone quay located probably twenty yards shy of the Marsh Farm buildings. At this point Sullivan gestured for me to stop. This was police work now. Sullivan and Thoroughgood were to knock on the front door with the other four policemen taking up positions, perhaps a chain distant from the building, in case of runners. Sullivan knocked heavily on the door and waited. Nothing. No sound, no light within, nothing. He did this again. On receiving no response this time, Thoroughgood dropped his bag and removed a heavy hammer and chisel out of it. He then slammed the hammer into the door lock and was much pleased to see splintering wood. He then jemmied the door with his chisel and in seconds they were in. I looked on expectantly. Time passed, still no noise from the inside, no raised voices, no nothing. Less than a minute later they emerged. Sullivan walked over to me.

"Sorry, Reeves. The place is empty. Some signs that people have been living there though."

I was gutted. What could I say? Had this all been a waste of time?

"But I saw a barge leaving the Ordnance Quay only yesterday."

Sullivan sniffed.

"That was probably them, sailing off into the sunset with Miss Pound on board."

We stood in silence. It was easy to feel forlorn, beaten. And then something took my eye.

"Look, over in the fort. There is a light coming from the room just above the land gate. I am going over there to take a look."

At that I set off at a fast pace. Sullivan reluctantly followed, as did his coterie of policeman. The land gate was reachable from Fort Road; I knew this because I had seen the cart take this very route yesterday. It involved going over a pair of old timber bridges that crossed the fort's outer moat defences, which had presumably been built to prevent attack from the landward side.

In no time we had arrived at the land gate. I could still see the light above it shining dimly through a small window at first-floor level. Sullivan looked awkward.

"I am not sure about this, Reeves. We are on military property now. I really need to check with the office about this."

I ignored him and gently pushed the gate. It was open, or at least ajar.

"I am going in."

The heavy gates pushed open inwards surprisingly easily. Then, just as I was about to speak to Sullivan I became aware of a taut wire connection from the gates to the roof, somewhere above my head. It could only be one thing.

"Watch out, it's a booby trap!" I yelled.

At that very moment a hatch opened in the room above, and a corpse, the body of a woman, dropped to the ground, just a few yards in front of me. Sullivan squealed.

"What the hell!"

For a few moments we all stood stunned but then unafraid of any other traps, I went over to the body. It could not be my Elisa! Please let it not be her!

I gingerly approached it. The face was head down. There was no doubt the girl was dead. I somehow found the strength and resolve to turn her over. For a second I shut my eyes, too scared of what I might have found. Then I opened them.

It was not Elisa. It was almost certainly the gypsy woman. The woman I had seen fighting with Romero at the prize fight.

I looked at Sullivan. Then from the depths of my memory I remembered something about this fort from my time in the Engineers.

"That room above is known as the dead room. When the Jacobites were imprisoned here in the 18th century the British troops garrisoned to guard them would dispose of their bodies by dropping them through the hatch, straight onto the back of a wagon to take them for burial, or disposal at least… I suppose Romero thinks this is funny."

The other policeman joined us and tried to arrange things around the corpse. No doubt there would have to be a post mortem.

Then at this point things turned from tragedy to farce. An old soldier walked, with a discernible limp, across the fort barrack square towards us. Presumably he had just got out of bed. We stood staring as he slowly made his way to us. He looked at us. He looked at the corpse. He was clearly shocked as well but trying to keep up appearances.

"What is going on here, gentlemen?"

Sullivan was clearly miffed.

"I was going to ask you the same thing. A body has just fallen out of the dead house through the trapdoor. What the hell is going on?"

The old soldier scratched his beard.

"Sorry, sir. No idea."

I could not just stand and watch this fiasco.

"So where is the rest of the garrison? Who is your commanding officer?"

He looked crestfallen.

"Sorry, sir. It is just me. The fort is mothballed at the moment. I am just the night watchman. An old soldier doing his duty."

"So who has been in the dead house? The woman couldn't just have wandered in there by herself."

He shuffled a bit.

"A couple of days ago chap from the Engineers turned up, said he had reports of a leaking roof in the barrel store. Told me that the ammunition needed to be taken away for storage elsewhere. He even arranged a barge and everything. He was definitely a sapper, had all the right paperwork and everything."

I was getting this sinking feeling.

"What did he look like?"

"He was a distinctive-looking gentleman; he had fought in Crimea like me. Definitely a Royal Engineer, no doubt about it."

"Anything else about him you remember?"

"Now you come to mention it, he had a big port-wine stain on…"

"That is enough. I don't need to hear anymore. You had better tell your superiors what has occurred. We have a murder scene here."

Sullivan piped up. "Thank you Reeves. You can leave this to me now."

I sloped off. The whole thing was a joke. Frankland was somehow still alive and with a bit of Crimean war banter and a few pieces of dodgy paperwork had got control of the barrel store, the munitions and the dead room above it. We had been taken for fools.

I trudged back across the moat bridges to Fort Road feeling distinctly downcast.

Before going back to the station I decided to do something positive and made a sortie back to Marsh Farm. The front door was still open of course as the police were now absorbed with the corpse in the fort, so I had the place to myself. Inside it was like any normal farmhouse with a parlour and living room, kitchen and outside privy. I immediately found the location in which the photographs of Elisa had been taken. The furnishings and wallpaper were distinctive enough. I wondered what the days spent here had been like for her. At least the need for regular photographs meant that she had been reasonably clothed and fed, no doubt; beyond that, who knows what might have occurred. I felt a wave of fear and repulsion. Caring for her made the thought of her imprisonment hard to take. I had to stay professional though and not let my anger overtake my judgement. Elisa was still out there somewhere, alive but probably very frightened. It was my job to find her and bring her back.

I trudged off along the road back to the riverside station. Luckily the station master was in and I was able to sit in his office. He kindly made some tea while I recounted what had occurred so far. When the stationmaster went out of the office to sort out an incoming train, he left me the morning's newspaper. I briefly skipped through it, finding concentration hard. However one story caught my attention. A headline: 'Heavy storms in the English Channel'. It went on… a number of boats had to seek shelter as a gale from the south-west swept up the Channel. It also affected boat traffic in the Thames estuary. Smaller boats have been particularly badly affected. Winds touching force nine on the Beaufort scale recorded.

I put the paper down. What if the *Rising Sun* barge had been caught up in that? What might have happened to her? I sat pensive, impatient for news, for someone to tell me what I should do next.

TWENTY-NINE

All at Sea, 26th September, Late Afternoon

Fifteen hours earlier, the *Rising Sun* had indeed found bad weather. It was now about six o'clock in the evening as the barge passed by Sheerness on the north-west point of the Isle of Sheppey. On board was the captain – Harry Houghton – an experienced man who had been on barges for thirty years, his second man was Able Audsley, still in his twenties but a hard worker. Below deck crammed up against the bow in the only space left over from the barrel storage were Henry Frankland, a young lady whose name he had not been told, and another Argentinean gentleman with a scarred face – Pedro.

Houghton had not wanted this job. Of course it paid well – Romero always did – but it broke all the rules. They were carrying explosives without the required red safety flags and would soon have to come into harbour as they were not allowed to sail at night. Added to this was that the weather was getting foul. A storm moving north-west up the Channel had now funnelled into the mouth of the Thames and was heading their way. They had not felt it until they had entered the open sea a few miles west of Sheerness but now the boat was bobbing like a cork. To add to his bad humour he could not light up his favourite pipe as matches were far too dangerous on an explosives barge. The barge was rolling badly, with the sails stretched and strained; at this rate he could break a mast. Houghton had strict orders to get the barge to a trig point about five miles north-east of Sheerness, so just beyond the Nore lightship and in international waters, which started two miles from the coastline. In international waters, the British Customs and Excise had no jurisdiction. Here they would rendezvous with the Argentinean steamship the *River Plate* which was sailing from Antwerp. How they were going to get the passengers and goods from one boat to the other was a challenge. In good weather on a placid sea, it might be possible, but in this storm! He looked to the south. He could see the lights of the Sheerness dockyard and the houses of the town, so he knew it was already darker than it should have been for the time of day. The harbourmaster at Sheerness would be wondering why the hell we were at sea in this weather. He would have to steel his nerves and tell Frankland the unpalatable truth. That was that liaising with the *River Plate* was impossible and dangerous.

Meanwhile down below, the three men and the lady were being pushed from pillar to post. The boat kept going up and down violently with the motion of the waves. The girl, Elisa, looked green with seasickness; only Frankland seemed unmoved. There was an almost manic glint in his eye. Almost as if he had a death wish.

Houghton came below manoeuvring himself through the narrow pathway created between the explosives barrels.

"Sorry, Mr Frankland. The storm is too vicious."

Frankland hardly paused before spitting out, "I am paying for this. You will do as I say."

Houghton stared back at him, looking a little lost. At that moment came the most tremendous crunching sound from above.

"I think we have a problem."

Houghton made his way back to the deck with great haste. The sight that greeted him was his main sail with the chain holding it taut snapped off, leaving the canvas blowing aimlessly in the gale force winds. Pretty soon the sails and rigging would be dragging along the water unless land could be made quickly. Frankland followed him up on deck.

"That is it then, sir; we have to make haste to get to land before we are swept away. Audsley, can you get us moving west towards shore? We may just be able to reach landfall. There is a jetty by the Grain Fort which nobody uses these days. We will tie up there for the night."

Frankland was spitting with anger. He was a man trapped by his own aggrandisement. He could see the sail hanging like a broken doll; he knew what it meant but still couldn't back down. Just then in the distance to the east he caught sight of the *River Plate*. It was also clearly rolling with the waves.

"Look, Houghton, only a mile or so away, surely we can make it?"

"It does not matter if it is one mile or a hundred, we can only go in the direction the winds take us now."

As if to echo his words a semaphore signal was coming from the *River Plate*. Frankland stood concentrating on the stuttering light through the stormy darkening sky.

Houghton clearly had encountered semaphore before and got the meaning.

Frankland barked, "What does it say?"

"Storm too strong. Heading for Sheerness…"

Frankland was incandescent with rage.

"Message him back. Tell him that he must not do that."

Houghton almost laughed.

"What do you think this is? HMS *Warrior*? I don't have a signal lamp to do semaphore. This is just a barge. I don't usually even leave the river, and I damn well wish I hadn't today!"

At this Houghton took over the helm from Audsley. Frankland fumed but it was testament to the man's skill that somehow, with a useless sail, he managed to nudge the boat towards land on the west bank of the Medway. Here it was all flat marshland – a lump of land called the Isle of Grain. Houghton knew this channel west of Sheerness was guarded by a Napoleonic Martello tower, half a mile out to sea, linked to the mainland by a raised track. Somehow he had to make sure the barge did not crash into it. The winds were pushing the boat in that direction and it took all his skill and experience to keep his craft away from the tower. But the danger was not over yet. Linking the tower to the mainland was a half-mile-long causeway, if the barge hit that it would be effectively wrecked. The craft was getting closer and closer, and then the inevitable happened, a rasping scraping sound. The barge had hit the rocky embankment on which the causeway sat. It was a nasty bang. For a moment

Houghton held his breath, but there was no sound of timber splintering. It looked as if the old timber barge had retained its integrity and just got cuts and bruises.

The wind abated for a minute or two, allowing the skipper to steer away from the causeway and crawl up the coastline in a northerly direction towards the Grain Fort jetty. It was another twenty minutes, but it felt like twenty hours, before the barge closed in on that isolated pier. Even then the danger was still paramount in their minds. How deep was the water lapping along the shoreline? What was underneath it? Could the timber of the jetty hold the barge in this storm? Through the driving rain the captain could see the D shaped fort, which was another of the relics from the Palmerston obsession with building defences along the Thames during the '60s.

As they got close to land, the strength of the sea decreased and somehow the captain was able to get the barge close to the modest jetty that had once served the fort. Houghton should have got a medal but all Frankland wanted was his blood.

Somehow Houghton managed to steer the barge alongside the quay and the second man, Audsley, jumped onto land to catch the hawser and safely tie the barge up. The skill of the bargemen was not to be underrated. All on board owed their lives to the thirty years' experience of the captain.

Frankland was the first ashore. He had worked on the Thames forts during their construction, so knew a little about them. He also seemed confident that the fort was no longer manned. Hopefully he could get them all inside the fort building, which should be out of the wind and a great deal drier. This was not ideal but he would have to make the best out of this dire situation.

Below deck things were less happy. Elisa was cold and damp and miserable and feeling the effects of seasickness. Pedro was little more than an animal. He would stare at her constantly, even when she had no option other than to use the chamber pot. She longed for release from this hell but it was now obvious that she would be a hostage to the very end. There was no sign of rescue, she had no idea where they were, or where they were going, or why. Being alone with this man was a constant worry; she knew perfectly well that it was only his fear of Frankland that had stopped him from trying to rape her.

The fort at Grain was perhaps a furlong distant from the jetty across the dead flat marsh with the land only raising itself as a bulwark to the fort outer walls. There was no habitation in front of the fort's walls to allow a clear range of fire for the artillery stationed within. Frankland knew a little of its background, it had been built in the 1860s but when Napoleon was deposed as French Emperor, it became pointless, so in recent years had been abandoned. This probably pleased the garrison as it truly was in the middle of nowhere surrounded by marshes and only accessible by boat, no doubt a thoroughly miserable place to be garrisoned.

Frankland was not put off by their plight.

"I'll get Pedro and the girl out of the hold. We will have to spend the night in the fort. At least there should be some shelter inside."

He looked at the immovable captain who looked less than happy.

"You too, Houghton."

The captain was having none of it.

"I and my first mate will be staying with the boat. I don't know what you gentlemen are up to but this adventure has cost me a pretty penny already and I don't intend to have my whole barge written off. I am staying with it."

Frankland could not bother to argue. He went below deck to extract Pedro and Elisa. They were soon out; probably hoping that being on dry land might ease their seasickness.

They got onto the pier as best they could and tried to keep their footing on the moss-covered timber decking. Then with the howling wind and rain soaking them to the bone they stumbled towards the fort. The track they took was obviously little used but thankfully short. Just shy of the fort walls was a deep hollow and they had to go down into that and up the slippery, steep pathway on the other side. Somehow they made it. They were soon up against the sturdy exterior walling; the curtain wall of the fort.

Frankland stalked around the perimeter wall like a dog sniffing out its prey. He soon found a partly broken timber door leading into the interior. They made their way into the darkness, and emerged in a windowless cavernous room with cold stone walls and not a stick of furniture to be seen. Frankland spoke.

"We are in the artillery magazine underneath where the guns are positioned. I would be surprised if we find much better. Perhaps Pedro could collect some wood and we can make a fire?"

He gestured for Pedro to obey. This was going to be a cold uncomfortable night. Luckily on the inside wall of the storeroom was a disused hearth. Unfortunately there was no sign of any coal or firewood detritus.

Within a few minutes Pedro had returned with what looked like broken crates and from these a fire was eventually started. The group were now able to dry themselves and their clothes. Elisa sat close to the fire. Pedro, to her discomfort, sat nearby. Frankland was restless and paced up and down the stone floor, occasionally finding some detritus to kick out of his way which then caused a cloud of unwanted dust to fill the room… He was in a foul mood. It was now deep into the evening and they were effectively trapped. Escape by boat was impossible and heading off across miles of uncharted marshland, probably lethal. His master plan ruined by of all things the unseasonable British weather. He cursed to himself.

Time moved on. It was now past midnight, then the early hours, but sleep eluded him. He would not be beaten. No way. His route to freedom was probably docked less than two miles away but at this moment it might as well have been on the other side of the earth.

Pedro was slumped in the corner, probably not asleep but feigning it. Elisa made no pretence. She was wide awake and clearly still terrified. Finally Frankland spoke.

"Pedro. I am going back to the barge; see if the men can make an emergency repair. You keep your eyes on her."

At that he left the room. The fire still smouldered giving some light and warmth to this spartan place.

With the Englishman gone Pedro seemed to come to life. He went over and shook Elisa. There was little need for that as she was fully awake, but he seemed to need to let her know who was in charge.

"I am tired of this, Rosina. Tired of being treated like a dog. I will get you away from here, and we can start a new life."

The words hung in the air. Elisa could not fathom how his mind was working.

"I am Elisa now. Rosina is ancient history. Why do you think I would want to go back there? Go back there with you. Anywhere with you?"

Pedro spat on the floor.

"You were my wife. As far as I am concerned you are still my wife. Why did you come to England if not to look for me?"

Elisa frowned. "I had no idea that you were in England. All I knew was that after the robbery. That robbery where you nearly killed me. You were on the run. I just assumed you would never be seen again. When Romero offered me a chance to go to England to work in his office I jumped at it. I wanted to leave you, my life, and my betrayal of the Hopes far behind me."

Pedro was not discouraged.

"But can't you see how fate has brought us back together? I too came to this country on one of Romero's boats. He gave me a position guarding his wharf. I have spent five long years there, hiding from the authorities, helping him with his business, and all the time you were only a few miles away from me. If only I had known. If only he had told me."

"It would have made no difference. I am a different person now. I would never have, never will, go back with you. You betrayed the family I worked for, your own boss, who treated you like one of the family. You are dead to me and when I get out of here I will go to the police. I will have you arrested and sentenced for the deaths you caused."

Pedro sat stunned. "If that is your final word, then I will have to kill you."

Elisa sniffed. "You would not have the nerve to look me in the eye and kill me. You are a coward."

"I am not a coward and I have killed before. Out on the marshes, I killed the boy, Fontaine."

She stared back at him with disbelief, speechless, finally the words came out.

"Why would you do that? Why would you kill someone so young? So innocent?"

"I was patrolling the land and I came upon him, he was writing or drawing something in a book. I looked at him and immediately knew he had recognised me, somehow he had remembered me from all that time ago in the hacienda. I had no choice. I hit him over the head and made it look as if he had been hit by the train. I was sorry I had to do that. He was young. But he would have told everyone where I was. My life would have been over."

Elisa looked at him with disgust.

"You pig. You killed a boy. You absolute, filthy pig."

Pedro looked at her, then away, and then walked up and down the room. She still had her hands shackled behind her back so could do nothing to harm him.

Finally he looked at her and spoke.

"I will kill you. Of that you can be sure. But before that I will claim my rights as a married man does with his legal wife."

At that he undid his heavy leather belt and dropped his trousers. Then, using both hands while kneeling on the floor, reached down to part her legs. Elisa looked terrified but was unable to do anything meaningful to resist. She stared up at the cold, dark ceiling and wondered what she had done to God to deserve this fate.

THIRTY

Tilbury Station, 27th September, Morning

EARLIER THAT SAME DAY, AT around nine o'clock, Reeves was still sitting in the stationmaster's office Tilbury, waiting for Sullivan to return. The monotony was broken when a train came in from London and the stationmaster went about his duties and Sullivan arrived at the door.

"Well we have been all over the fort. Seems that the corpse was laid over the hatch, soon as the land gate was opened it pulled a wire that opened the hatch, and Bob's your uncle."

"Why would they do that?"

Sullivan sniffed.

"And why did he leave a lantern on to lure us to the fort? They are trying to make fools out of us."

I hardly knew how to respond. The opposition did indeed seem two steps in front of us all the time. We sat for a few minutes saying little then something happened to dispel the air of gloom: a breath of fresh air. The avuncular face of Bill Barrington appeared at the office door. Sullivan gestured him to come in.

"Sorry, Reeves. Detective Sullivan. I had to be part of the action."

I smiled.

"Sit down, you silly sod."

"I have not been idle though. I've been round the city first thing this morning and got some useful information. It appears that the *River Plate* left Antwerp first thing yesterday morning, destination Bama in the Congo delta."

"Just as we thought," I said. Bill nodded.

"Even more interestingly, it seems to have got into trouble in the storm overnight and is now sitting in Sheerness dockyard."

I could hardly contain my pleasure.

"That is great news. We still have a chance of getting Romero and saving Elisa before he gets onto the high seas."

Bill was beaming.

"And there's more. My contact at Sheerness has seen a sailing barge, probably the *Rising Sun* moored up outside Grain Fort, about a mile and a half across the Medway from him."

Sullivan was listening to every word intently. He joined the conversation.

"I think I have heard enough now. I will message the harbourmaster at Sheerness to get Romero's boat impounded to stop her leaving."

Sullivan spoke to the stationmaster who then telegraphed under his direction. A few minutes later he was back.

"That is done then. I think we might have Romero in the net, and where he is, Elisa will not be far away."

We were treated to warming cups of tea. The morning had started as a farce but now, with luck, we might have the edge over Romero at last.

I then turned to Sullivan. "So, what can I do to help matters?"

Sullivan pulled a long face.

"Reeves, I'm afraid nothing would be the best thing you could do. This is a matter for the police and the harbourmaster. We will liaise with the Excise people and hopefully get onto the ship to give it a full search. At the same time we should be able to bring Romero in for questioning, so it looks as if it's job done."

I sat quietly, I was not so sure.

"And, what about the barge? If it's moored across the river by the fort they may have Elisa with them. How do we get to her?"

Sullivan stroked his chin.

"Tricky one that, Reeves. My guess is though that as soon as the weather improves it will make a dash for Sheerness Harbour and try and rendezvous with the *River Plate*. That might be our chance to get Elisa back and arrest those holding her."

I was less than pleased with this but wanted to keep Sullivan on side at all costs.

"Very well, I will leave the matter in your hands."

Sullivan nodded.

"Good. Best thing you can do is go home and get some sleep. I'll keep you informed of what transpires."

The London bound train was leaving in a couple

of minutes so I shook Sullivan's hand, thanked the stationmaster, and with Bill in tow made my way onto the platform. The train soon came and we were soon whisking through the marshy Essex countryside back to town. Bill could sense my disappointment. He was never a man to keep his feelings to himself.

"So, I can see you're miserable. What do you want to do about it? We cannot leave this just to the police can we?"

"What can we do? I have no powers to arrest Romero, or any of his gang, and as to maritime law and Excise matters, I probably know less than you."

We sat glumly for the rest of the journey.

I was home well before noon. I should have been content at the progress so far but nagging doubts were filling my mind. I was restless. I pored through my collection of newspapers and periodicals looking for anything on the Congo.

It didn't take long to find numerous articles of interest. It appeared that the Belgium king, Leopold II, was hell bent on creating a new empire in Africa to rival Britain. His chief area of interest was the lands around the River Congo and to this end he was employing the famous American explorer, Henry Morton Stanley, to survey the area. Stanley also had a contract with the *Daily Telegraph* newspaper, to report on his adventures. If nothing else this proved that there would be big money available to people like Romero, who could provide shipping to service the Congo survey. It was clear from the articles that Britain and Belgium were to some extent rivals in this. Both countries, and other nations like France, Germany and Portugal, were also trying to colonise the remaining lands in Africa which nobody had claimed.

However despite this rivalry I noticed that Leopold had a family link to Queen Victoria. One wondered how this affected the relationship between the countries. There was a lot to think about here but the only thing truly on my mind was Elisa, and her fate.

I was awakened from my pit of depression by a knock at the door. I quickly opened it and it was a telegram boy. I took the message, gave him a tip and read its contents in seconds. It was from Edward Hope. He was in England staying at Aunt Matilda's. Could I get over to see him immediately? I needed no further prompt. I quickly put on my hat and coat and hailed a cab. By late afternoon I was at Matilda's front door in Horndon.

THIRTY-ONE

Grain Fort, the Night of 26th and 27th September

PEDRO WAS FULLY AROUSED AND now dragging on her pantaloons. Soon, very soon, he would have what he had longed for. She was small and weak compared with him… She stood no chance. Then suddenly a slight breeze ruffled the still dank air. Frankland appeared at the door. Within seconds he had guessed what was occurring.

Pedro stared at him.

"She is my wife; I am taking what I am owed for all these years."

She turned to Frankland.

"He is a monster. That woman at the fort, the gypsy woman, he raped her before killing her. That is the sort of man he is."

Scarcely had the words left her mouth, when Frankland pulled out a revolver and in one move shot Pedro through the heart. Blood and guts splattered over Elisa. Pedro slumped onto her, a dead weight. Frankland pulled his body aside.

There was coldness about Frankland; perhaps it was his military training. Calmly he dragged the body across the floor to the timber door. Using his shoulder he opened the door and half dragged, half carried the body through. He was back in a few minutes. His clothes now had bloodstains everywhere. He rubbed his hands together and wiped something off them. Elisa looked at him.

"What have you done with the body?"

"You don't need to concern yourself about that. I've done a good job."

She looked at him still in shock. He was now standing more upright and full of confidence.

"One good thing about working on these forts – you know where to hide the bodies. Might be a while before he is found."

He then wandered off again and this time came back with two crates. He gestured for her to sit on one. He sat on the other.

"That's better than the stone floor isn't it."

He seemed almost chirpy now. Elisa was beginning to realise that he was not mentally stable. Perhaps the pox had affected his brain. They sat in silence for quite a time. Both of them had Pedro's blood on their clothes and skin but there was precious little that could be done about that.

Elisa found this place chilling but Frankland seemed almost at home, for a man who seemed to work with ordnance all his life perhaps a munitions store was his natural home from home. Finally he spoke.

"No good Argie bastard. Glad to see the back of him."

He waited for some assurance from Elisa but none was forthcoming. He shuffled nervously on the crate which had become his seat.

"Must be hard for a fine-looking woman like yourself. Having to fend off creeps like him?"

He waited for a response but got none.

"Foreigners, all the same, but a good English lad like me. A man who appreciates a fine-looking woman like yourself. That is a different thing altogether."

He reached out and touched her dishevelled skirt and gently undid the creases.

"Now that bastard has been seen off perhaps you might look more kindly towards me. Give me some respect. See that I saved you from a fate worse than death. Maybe give something back to me as a thank you."

He reached out and stroked her exposed calf.

Elisa had had enough.

"You disgust me. I would no more go with you than a rabid dog. Take your filthy eyes and filthy hands off me."

"Only like the Argie type, do you? Filthy, dirty foreigners. All black hair and oily moustaches. Is that what excites you? You are a fucking ungrateful bitch. I should have known. You are all the same. I gave everything to Mary, even bought her a lovely pub. It was a licence to print money. And what does she do? What does that whore do when I'm down the salt mine, slogging my guts out to make money for her? I'll tell you what. She is taking men round the back of the pub into the shed and letting them fuck her. Slag, whore! And you know what? You know what? She ended up getting a dose of the pox. Served her right, but then the bitch passed it onto me."

There was an awkward silence. It went on for quite some time. Elisa had nothing to say to him and he had spent most of his pent-up anger. Finally after several minutes she spoke.

"So what do you want? What is the point of all this?"

"The point is that I deserve a new life, and I am going to get it. We are going to cross the river at first light and get onto Romero's boat. He is taking me to the Congo in Africa… I don't know what he wants from you. Probably got a nice little hacienda in the Argentine lined up where you can play happy families. But then you wouldn't say no to him, a swarthy Diego with money in every pocket, would you. A pretty girl like you, not as young as you were though, you'll be easy pickings for a man with his wealth."

Elisa tried her best to hit back.

"You don't know me at all. How dare you presume that I will be easy?"

No response came from Frankland, another silence loomed. She thought it wise to fill it.

"In any case. Why are you going to the Congo? What is there in that place for you?"

He perked up.

"Anything and everything I want. Lots of money, easy money, and all the women I could ever need. Ten a penny they are when they see a well-healed white man. Do anything you want I'm told."

"But you've got the pox."

"They won't know that. Why should I care? Like I say, they are ten a penny."

"So why not let me go? You've got it all planned out. Just release me and I'll forget about everything that's occurred.

I won't mention what you did to Pedro. You will be in the clear. A free man."

"You are so naïve. When I take the barge across the river I need you on board. And do you know why? Because if it is just myself, an old army man, and the crew; the navy will just blow us out of the water. You see, my dear, thirty years' service to Queen and country, counts for nothing. Keeping a frigid wife clothed and fed for years means nothing. But you, Miss Princess perfect, a nice young lady who has a respectable position in a London office. They wouldn't lay a glove on you, let alone shoot you out of the water. And, of course, our mutual friend Mr Romero wants you alive. So whether you like it or not, you're coming."

Elisa was struggling for words.

"But this is so unfair. What have I done to you for you to hate me so much?"

"You and your kind, look down their noses at me. A man who has kept this country safe, years in the Royal Engineers, a decade at the Royal Arsenal breathing in all those foul chemicals. And I am still nothing. A nobody. Even when I find what I think is a good woman, she turns out to be a whore. So I am going where the women are not so picky, and my ticket there relies on you staying alive… for now."

Frankland sat back on his crate and reached into his pocket for his hip flask. A big slug of that and he went quiet. Now he just sat and stared at her for an interminable time. His eyes had nothing but disdain and envy in them. It was going to be a long night.

Neither of them had any sleep. How Frankland stayed awake was beyond Elisa. Finally at dawn he disappeared, presumably going down to the barge. Perhaps one way or another the hell would soon be over. There was no such luck. Within the hour he had returned in a foul mood. The barge was still unable to sail it appeared. He brought out some paltry provisions which no doubt he had purloined from the crew.

"Here you are. Not much. I had not planned for us to be stuck here. We should be halfway across the Channel by now." She said nothing but took the proffered food. He said little. Just spent the day pacing up and down the room. It seemed that the madness that was seemingly engulfing him was fuelling his energy. His only concession to civilisation was to leave the area when Elisa had to use the pot. He was also clearly unwilling to release her.

The day dragged on. Now and again he would leave the room and climb to the walls of the fort and check the horizon. But nothing. Clearly there was no rescue mission for her. It was now late afternoon and hunger and tiredness and the cold were really beginning to affect her. Why wasn't she being rescued? Why didn't the Royal Navy come for her? Despair was setting in.

THIRTY-TWO

Horndon,
27th September, Afternoon

IT WAS INDEED GOOD TO see Edward Hope again. It seemed he was in the country on a scheduled visit but had word from contacts that trouble was afoot with Romero. He had also been tipped off by a friend at Sheerness that the *River Plate* was in harbour. I filled him in with all the events that had occurred since I last saw him and thanked him profusely for Matilda's help providing this information that helped me raid Scrivener's photographic workshop. Finally we got to the nub of the discussion. Hope looked me in the eye.

"My understanding is that the *River Plate* was initially impounded at Sheerness but a little bird tells me that politics may take a hand. It appears that Romero is on some mission from King Leopold of Belgium to survey the Congo region. Aided and abetted by the American explorer Stanley. As Leopold is a cousin of Queen Victoria my guess is that by tomorrow that situation will change and the *River Plate* allowed to sail."

I nodded and added my concerns.

"To complicate matters a barge full of explosives is lying across the water from Sheerness at the empty Grain Fort jetty, and on board are Romero's explosive expert, Frankland, and the hostage, Miss Elisa Pound." Hope looked concerned and took some deep breaths before speaking.

"This Miss Pound, she is the woman he has held captive for several weeks already?" There was an awkward atmosphere. Matilda went out to the kitchen to get more biscuits.

"I am going to have to tell you something. Something I should have told you at the start. Elisa Pound is not her real name. That was Rosina; she worked for my grandson in the Argentine."

I was dumbstruck, he sensed my frustration.

"She came over to England to start a new life. I was still on good terms with Romero then, so getting her work in his London office seemed a good result for all concerned. We decided it would be in her best interest to take on an English name, as her ex-partner, Pedro, was still on the run and might try and find her… Sorry, I should have told you this at the start."

Hope was clearly a man of business and before I could come to terms with this he had carried on.

"So what we need is a plan of action to save Elisa from Frankland and stop them getting on board the *River Plate*, if that is their idea. If we can do that perhaps we will have enough evidence to stop Romero from leaving harbour and we can arrest the lot of them."

I agreed with this summary of events and the course of action.

"So how do we go about it?"

Hope smiled. "I have a good friend with a boat that is moored at Stanford Wharf. He is a fine sailor and should be able to get you over to Grain Fort to see what you can do."

I was torn by indecision on this.

"There is nothing I would like more than to confront Frankland and rescue Elisa but surely this is a matter for the police or the navy. We should not be taking the law into our own hands."

Hope looked displeased. "Reeves, the one thing I've learnt in my long life is that you sometimes have to do just that. If we wait for the police to sort out the politics of it all, we shall literally miss the boat. You understand?"

"Quite."

Hope beamed.

"Good. You will need some help. I am too old to be of much use but that lad who helped you with Scrivener – Jamie Baldwin – I'll get him to come along with you."

I shook my head.

"That is very kind but I cannot use a young lad on such a dangerous mission."

Hope looked at me, then Matilda. There was something unsaid in the room.

"Hard to tell you this Reeves, but Jamie is not just the blacksmith's son, he is…" He gathered his words carefully.

"Elisa's son."

The words hit me like a sword through the guts. I sat staring for a few seconds unable to form the words.

"But how?"

Hope now took his time to answer. Clearly the subject still hurt him.

"It goes back to the time that Romero and myself were still partners. He came to me, told me Rosina had gone off the rails. Lost her mind and had been sent to a lunatic asylum. So he brought the boy here, said he was now de facto an orphan, and could we help? Well I could not say no. Matilda kindly looked after the rest. Paid the blacksmith to adopt him and give him a new name."

There was an awkward silence in the room that Hope finally filled.

"Of course we realise now that we were tricked and Romero was using us to get his own back on the girl. Sorry about all that. I should have told you the full story straight away."

I felt stumped. Lost for words.

"Does Jamie know about his birth mother?"

Matilda spoke.

"No. And we would be grateful if you can keep it to yourself."

Edward added, "It could traumatise the lad. Let us keep the truth from him for a while longer."

I was still fuming.

"And her?"

Matilda spoke apologetically, "And her, of course."

Bizarrely, Matilda started pouring some more tea from the pot. Hope though was ready to put things into motion.

"Good. Then get yourself and Jamie down to Stanford Creek. It will be almost dark before you get onto the Thames but my friend Jack is a fine sailor. He will get you downriver to Grain Fort this side of midnight."

I nodded.

"What will you be doing Edward?"

"I am going back to Westminster. Have a few words at Scotland Yard and see if any of the politicians can be of use. Probably see you in Sheerness."

At that I left. This was going to be a tough mission but Elisa's life probably depended on me getting it done.

THIRTY-THREE

Sailing to Freedom, 27th September, Early Morning

FRANKLAND WAS LIKE A TWITCHING wreck. Emotions such as anger and frustration seemed to be competing inside his head. Morning had broken but still things were unchanged. Elisa still sat motionless, her face a picture of misery. He had suffered enough.

"I am going to check on the barge again."

He came over to her and tightened the bindings that kept her imprisoned.

"I will not be long."

At that he stormed off. Outside the air was fresh, autumn was coming early. He could see the *Rising Sun* still moored against the jetty, its mainsail just a broken mess. There was no sign of activity on the Sheerness side of the river but he could see the *River Plate* still docked close to the harbour quay. He reached the jetty and noted that Houghton and Audsley were still working.

"Any progress?"

Houghton looked an embittered man.

"My boat's a bloody wreck. I should never have tried to ride that storm. There will be a pretty penny to pay when all this is over."

Frankland sniffed.

"All I need is from you is to get myself and Miss Pound over those two miles of water to the *River Plate*, then your work is done. So stop moaning. How long before it's seaworthy?"

Houghton sighed, looked up and down the rigging on the masts, and then responded.

"If you just need it to go as far as Sheerness dock it might be possible that we can get her ready by late afternoon. We will have to brail the mainsail to the mast and use the topsail and headsail only. With luck we should be able to get across the river with just those if the tide is with us."

Frankland almost smiled.

"Good, that is what I needed to hear. We will wait till it's dark though, just in case the navy wants to play silly buggers. So we will aim to leave at six thirty."

It was an order not a suggestion.

"You know it's illegal for a barge to be sailing at night don't you?"

Frankland could hardly contain his venom.

"Stop thinking like some sad old boatman, I have this."

He brandished his revolver.

"And a hostage. We go when I say."

Houghton said nothing but his look said everything. Audsley just stayed quiet. He knew this man was off his head.

"Very well. Six thirty it is and as soon as we make the harbour jetty over there, we are off. We're not hanging about."

"Very well. And don't have any ideas about leaving without me."

"Of course not, sir."

Frankland was unconvinced.

"In fact as a little insurance I am going to set up a little explosive device with a timer on it. You leave without me, and any second you could be blown to kingdom come. Do I make myself clear?"

"Very well, sir."

Frankland went into the hold, presumably to set up the time bomb. Audsley and Houghton busied themselves with the emergency repairs to the rigging. A few minutes later he emerged.

"Alright, that is done. Do not mess with it! I will see you men later."

At that he strode off the boat and made haste to the fort.

The rest of the day was a continuation of the night. Frankland stared at Elisa for long periods, and then ran up to the ramparts to check on the horizon and any sign of activity from the barge or the *River Plate* across the waters. Nothing of note occurred. The day dragged on. Hunger was now becoming an issue but he had his hip flask to keep him warm. Though the brandy was fast disappearing.

Finally at six Elisa was dragged to her feet, still bound with her hands behind her back. They walked out of the fort down to the jetty. Elisa at the front stumbling on the wet grass and now clearly weakened by her captivity.

Within a few minutes she was on the boat with Frankland, and the crew were ready to cast off. He looked at the sky, the weak sunset had now gone completely, and darkness had fallen. It was time to make their escape.

THIRTY-FOUR

The Yawl, 27ᵗʰ September – Late Afternoon

We reached the mooring point for the yawl *Betsy* at Stanford Creek at 6p.m. The owner of the yawl, Jack Johnson, was waiting for us. A middle-aged man with a firm handshake, he was willing to take part in a risky operation, just on the say so of his friend Edward Hope. A true friend indeed.

It was now getting dark and there was a chill wind in the air. I was a little unsettled about our journey across the Thames and what we would find at Grain Fort. Ideally I would have liked days to plan all this but I had no choice other than to grab the essentials: warm clothing, a Davy lamp and a little food and water, and get on with it. Edward had also provided me with a revolver. I prayed that I would not need to use this in anger.

We set off from the creek shore and into the darkness of the lower Thames. We were set on an east-south-easterly course and the tide was in our favour. Notwithstanding this there was obviously an ever-present risk of big ships crossing our path. We would scarcely be visible to them and even their washes could turn us over if we got close. It made me realise what a favour Jack was doing for us.

I turned towards Jamie. He was beaming; this was clearly the adventure he had always wanted.

We made steady progress. Although sparsely populated there were enough properties near the river with lights on to ratify our direction of travel. We passed the Chapman lighthouse to port, and then sailed in a south-easterly direction through the middle of the river before reaching the relative calm of the waters off the Kent bank. I noted the hamlet of Allhallows, on the south bank. We were now out of the main shipping lane and hugging the north Kent coastline, following the edge of the marshland east from Allhallows towards Grain Fort. Jack was a very experienced sailor and made our journey almost effortless, even in the darkness.

I became aware though that Jamie was now very quiet and withdrawn. I smiled at him. "Everything alright, Jamie? Are you warm enough?"

"I am fine, sir." He hesitated then continued. "Excuse me for asking, sir, but you are a friend of Mr Hope and the man we are after is an Argentinean. Is that right?"

"Indeed."

"The thing is, something funny happened a while back at the forge. This man, who people said was from the Argentine, turned up in Horndon asking questions."

I let the silence break his words but was happy to hear him continue.

"Anyway the man came to the forge. Said he was looking for his son. Pa made me hide around the back so he couldn't see me. I got sight of him though. Proper dark he was, with a scar on his face. Seems he was working on Mister Romero's farm on the marshes."

I had to be careful in my response.

"So why did that worry you?"

Jamie looked into the palms of his hands.

"Just seemed funny that's all. Don't make no sense. Anyway Pa told him there was nobody he knew that could be his son, and the man went away."

I was in no hurry to respond but then calmly said, "he was probably just after money. I would forget about it."

That seemed to settle the matter for now. We went back to our jobs of scanning the coastline.

Soon we could see the outline of the fort to the south and a small jetty in front of us. It was now seven o'clock. The jetty was empty – which must mean that the barge had left already. That was not what I had expected. We pulled in close and I jumped off and fastened the mooring ropes.

Leaving Jack on board, myself and Jamie walked up to the fort, lantern in hand. We soon found, even in the darkness, the broken doorway. We entered and found the remains of recent habitation. Bits of firewood, a full chamber pot. Then I noticed something more chilling, there was blood in the centre of the room splattered onto the dusty floor. The blood then smeared across the floor towards what looked like an opening to the rear of the magazine floor. Jamie looked at me. He was thinking what I was. Had Elisa met her end here in this cold lonely hell hole? We followed the blood smearing out into the open air through a narrow gap between brambles.

There was less blood here but signs of crushed vegetation that we followed. There could only be one explanation: a body or someone badly wounded had been dragged out here. Alongside the rear stone wall of the fort was a ditch, a sort of primitive moat. Inside it and staring up were the eyes on a dead man's head, a corpse. I could immediately see the path of the bullet which had hit him right in the chest, almost certainly close enough to the heart for death to be immediate. We looked at his face. He was undoubtedly a man of Latin stock probably Argentine – almost certainly Pedro. We looked at each other, both of us appalled at finding a dead body but also relieved that it was not Elisa.

I spoke first.

"Looks as if the gang fell out. This man has been shot dead. No doubt about it."

I held his wrist for a moment looking for the pulse that no longer was.

"Dead, no doubt about it. Let's leave this and get back to the boat. This must mean that Elisa and Frankland must be on the barge."

Jamie looked frozen in fear, the colour drained from his face. Perhaps he had never seen a dead body before.

"That's him. That's the man who came to the forge."

I kept quiet. If the Argentinean was Jamie's father, the less said the better.

I had no desire to hang around this God-awful place any longer than needed.

"I am sure you are mistaken. It is easy to jump to conclusions. Let us get back to the boat. We cannot do any good here."

At that we retraced our steps and returned to the jetty,

both of us were shocked and our mouths dry. I had seen dead bodies before, going right back to Crimea, but it still affected me.

Jack was still sitting on his boat perusing Sheerness Harbour across the river through his telescope.

"What can you see?" I ventured.

He handed me the telescope. Even in the dark I could make out, through the lights on shore, the outline of the *River Plate* lying at anchor. This was on the north side of the main pier that jutted out into the Medway on an east-west axis. Harder to see, but discernible just, was a barge, almost certainly the 'Rising Sun' on the south side of the pier. So that is where they were now. I turned to Jack.

"Let us get over to Sheerness." Without a word he cast off. Soon we would be within yards of my greatest enemy and my greatest love.

THIRTY-FIVE

The Rising Sun
27th September, Early Evening

THERE WAS NOT A GOOD atmosphere on the *Rising Sun*. The skipper was fighting to keep the boat on the only safe route across the Medway. Frankland just stood scowling, sometimes pointing his revolver at Elisa's head for no good reason other than to keep the crew on their toes. They knew one false move and he would willingly kill them all. It was dark, too dark for comfort but Frankland would not allow the lantern to be lit... He wanted the barge to cross the river undetected at all costs. They only had the lights from Sheerness dockyard to show them the way. *The River Plate* was in view now; tied up on the north side of the pier which had a large safety beacon at its extremity.

The wind began to get up. Houghton was struggling to steer the barge; it was being sucked into the shore by the prevailing easterly wind and tides. Frankland sensed this.

"I need you to get alongside the *River Plate*."

The captain looked at him in despair.

"I will not be able to get us around the pier; we will have to dock on the south side."

Frankland fumed. "That is not good enough."

Houghton was getting angry himself.

"If you can do any better, you try helming. It is either dock on the south side of the pier or crash into the seawall. One or the other?"

Frankland was incandescent.

"Whatever!"

Even achieving this was not easy. Somehow, just using the remaining sails, they had got this far. The captain was glad that the barge had a shallow draught; most boats would already be scraping along the beach by now. But they made it. The barge bumped against the timber pier. Audsley jumped up onto it and had soon fastened fore and aft ropes to the iron supports which ran the length of the pier. They had made it.

Within seconds a man had appeared through the darkness and began shouting at them.

"What are you doing, sailing at night? You cannot moor here. What the hell are you doing?"

Frankland looked at the man. Houghton was silent. He pointed the gun at Elisa's head.

"Go and get the harbourmaster. Now. And tell him this barge is full of high explosives. Any funny business and the dockyard will go up. Do I make myself clear?"

The man, now clearly out of his depth, scurried away.

A few minutes later a well-dressed gentleman appeared. Clearly ruffled but in control, he spoke slowly but strongly, his voice carrying from shore to boat.

"I believe you asked for the harbourmaster. I am he, Jacob Smith, at your service. What do you want?"

Elisa looked on. She could see more lights being lit onshore. Clearly the word that trouble was afoot was now doing the rounds of Sheerness. Frankland spoke clearly and loudly enough to be heard by all.

"I believe you have the Argentinean vessel, the *River Plate*, in dock here. I am requesting the captain to bring his ship around to this side of the pier and tow us out of harbour. Once we are outside the three-mile limit the crew and the young lady, and the barge, will be released and you can do with them as you see fit."

The harbourmaster was clearly in a state of turmoil but doing his best to look in charge of the situation.

"I will need to speak to the Excise and the admiralty before I can give permission for the *River Plate* to sail."

Frankland grimaced.

"I have a time bomb at my disposal. A device with enough power to ignite the rest of the explosives on this boat. You see, I have the edge over you, over everyone here. And you know why? Because I don't care if I live or die! Setting the bomb off will be my pleasure, but your precious Royal Naval dockyard of Sheerness will be blown apart. That will not be too good for your career… that is in the unlikely event of you still being alive."

Jacob had now got the message loud and clear. "I will be as quick as I can. Don't do anything silly."

Frankland almost laughed as he scurried away. Now

it was just a waiting game. He looked at his pocket watch – seven thirty. Elisa was still by his side at the end of the revolver, shaking slightly, whether through the evening chill, or fear, he did not know. Houghton spoke.

"Now he is on the dock, what about letting Audsley go? You only need one man to helm this craft if we are under tow. I can do that."

Frankland thought for a moment.

"Very well, but on condition he goes over to the *Plate* and speaks to the captain and the ship owner, Mr Romero."

Houghton nodded.

"He can do that."

Frankland turned to the second hand who had been standing on the pier since securing the hawsers. "Tell the captain that I need him to bring his ship around, fasten a line to this boat and tow us out to sea; tell him the harbourmaster will be agreeing to this."

Houghton gestured for Audsley to get a move on. He did not need any encouragement and disappeared off in the direction of the Argentinean ship.

Now all went quiet again. There was nothing to say. Both Houghton and Elisa were keeping quiet for fear of his temper. It was an awkward all-encompassing silence only broken by some sound from the ramparts of the nearby garrison. As expected the soldiers had been roused and were now finding positions where they could take a pot shot at Frankland. He seemed unconcerned at this possibility; he knew that as long as the time bomb was in his hands, he had all the aces up his sleeve.

THIRTY-SIX

Sheerness,
27th September, Evening

JUST ACROSS THE PIER SAT the *River Plate* in all her glory. Her captain was a gentleman by the name of Ricardo Fernandez, an experienced sailor, who knew his way around the seven seas. More importantly he knew that Alfonso Romero owned the shipping line and he must agree to all his whims, if he wanted to keep his exalted position.

They had been stuck in Sheerness for over twenty-four hours now and the threat of the ship being impounded felt very real. So it was with some surprise that the captain staring out from his position on the bridge saw the Thames barge docking at the pier. It was not a comfortable watch; clearly the barge had lost its main sail so all the sailing was being done with the hastily patched-up remnants. He looked at the deck of the barge through his binoculars. Even in the limited light he could see what appeared to be a man who was holding a gun to the head of a lady, whilst the seaman helming the barge and his mate were engrossed in keeping the tub afloat. He put the binoculars down.

Romero appeared by his side.

"Well, Ricardo, it looks as if our barge has made it after all. My guess is that Frankland will be requesting a tow from us. You had better tell the engine room to make some steam. We could be leaving here very shortly."

"I thought we were impounded?"

"Just paperwork, Ricardo, empty words. The barge is full of dynamite. There is no way the harbourmaster will let it be moored here for a second longer than necessary. Towing her out is the only safe option. Which would work out very nicely as once we get past the three-mile limit, they cannot touch us."

Romero smiled, the captain looked uneasy.

"Towing a barge like that, with so much explosive, it is, shall we say, undesirable. If it blows up, so do we. It breaks all the rules of the sea."

Romero looked at the captain with disdain.

"Do not quote rules of the sea to me. I own this shipping line. This ship. We have an important mission to take the dynamite to the Congo. We have been specially selected by King Leopold to do this. So don't tell me it's unethical or dangerous. I know what needs to be done, and you're doing it."

Ricardo stood quietly for a moment, and then reached for the tube's speaker.

"Engine room. Get the steam up now. We will leave imminently."

Romero stood back. This was all working out very well after all.

Meanwhile Jack's yawl had now manoeuvred out into the middle of the Medway and those on board could see the events unfurling at Sheerness. It was now seven forty-five. The *River Plate* had lights on so the silhouette of the ship was clearly visible. Just then a signal light could be seen flashing from the bridge of the ship. I nudged Jack and pointed to the flashing light.

"What is he saying?"

Jack took his time and waited for the signal to fully finish.

"Coming around to you now. Will throw out tow rope. Be ready to fasten."

We looked at each other. So it was going to tow the barge out of the harbour. If they succeeded in this they could be out at sea beyond the three-mile limit within the hour. Jack looked at me. "What do you want to do?"

"We have to stop them. Take the boat as close as we can to the barge without being spotted. Then we will play it by ear." Jack grimaced but agreed. We were playing a dangerous game but had gone too far now to stop.

We could see the *River Plate* clearly beyond the pier making steam. Before too long she was moving, the hawsers had been thrown on board, and she was heading off. Somehow my eyes had adjusted to the half-light and I could see more clearly the ship's movements. It had now moved about a furlong or two out from the shoreline, and then started to edge to port. It was clearly aiming to go around the pier end before getting into the right position to throw a towline to the barge.

I had brought my binoculars and so trained these on the barge. It was difficult to see in the darkness but I could just make out three people. Frankland with the gun, Elisa being held close to him and presumably the barge captain standing a little distance away. By the look of it, the harbourmaster had caved in and allowed the ship to leave, perhaps under duress. We could see this all, but how could we intervene?

Our yawl was still a fair distance from the barge. Jack was holding the boat firm with as little movement as possible in case this caught the moonlight on the waves. We sat in complete darkness impotent to intervene.

On the pier the harbourmaster reappeared and shouted out to the men on the barge.

"Very well. I have permission to agree to your demands. The ship will tow you out to sea and we will not intervene, but…" He continued…

"Make no mistake, the full weight of British justice will fall on you for your behaviour here today. Mark my words."

Frankland looked him up and down slowly. Then said one word. "Prat!"

At this, the harbourmaster scowled. He was clearly furious. Frankland laughed maniacally. Then looked beyond the pier to the ship now making its way towards them, and addressed his captives.

"Here she comes. All you have to do, Houghton, is catch the hawser and make it taut. Then take the helm." He turned to Elisa.

"Not long now, and this will all be over."

He then turned back to the harbourmaster and Audsley standing on the dockside; they had now been joined by port workers and soldiers.

He shouted at them. "Do not try to intervene! I have a time bomb at my fingertips. If I am shot, or in any way attacked, I will lose my hold on the trigger mechanism, and it will blow up this barge, and half of Sheerness with it!"

The men on the quay looked at each other. Worry was etched into their faces.

The next few minutes seemed like a lifetime. The *River Plate* was now backing, stern first, towards the barge. Then a hawser was thrown and caught by Houghton who had swiftly tied it securely to the bow of the barge.

Frankland seemed intoxicated by his own power. Clearly as a man who had endured thirty years of taking orders from his betters, this was his finest hour. Almost immediately the Argentinean ship began moving forward, towing the barge. It hardly needed helming but Houghton took charge of that. The ship was making steam and with its powerful engines made light work of pulling them.

I was at a loss as to what to do. Going ashore and arguing with the harbourmaster would probably be futile. It would be beyond his powers to intervene. The only option was to follow the ship, and the barge being towed out to sea, and hope that they would move slowly enough for the yawl to keep them in sight. Jack immediately agreed this course of action but we both knew that a small sailing boat would be no match for a steamship. The leading boats headed out of the Medway channel into the estuary. Probably aware that high speeds might break the tow rope, the ship was going at a steady but unspectacular pace. The lights from the *River Plate* made them easy to follow. The wind was from the west, thus pushing us towards starboard, so Jack had to gently correct this movement.

It was soon clear that they were getting away from us. A furlong gap turned into two, then more. This was futile but our only hope was that the ship would stop beyond the three-mile limit and the *Plate* would endeavour to load the explosives off the barge. In itself that would be highly dangerous and with Frankland on board, anything could happen. I certainly had no doubt that in his mental state he was perfectly willing to blow himself, and everyone else, up on a whim.

The gap widened perhaps four or more furlongs – at half a mile we were just keeping eyes on the ship and barge. Luckily it was a clear moonlit night; otherwise we would have been stuffed. Then, what I hoped for happened, the *River Plate* began to slow, imperceptibly at first, then more markedly, bringing both boats to an almost stationary state, bobbing in the light swell. This gave us a chance to get closer.

Romero and Fernandez were orchestrating things from the bridge. The seventy-fathom-long towrope was pulled in and the barge sidled up to the bigger ship. Houghton was a skilled mariner and brought the barge alongside the ship without fuss. The crew of the ship threw cargo nets over the side and onto the deck of the barge, followed by a rope ladder.

From the yawl we watched all this with mounting concern. Surely Romero would not try and move the explosives here and now, the risks were too much. I could now make out the outline of Elisa. It looked as if she was tied to the main mast and unable to move.

We got closer. Then I saw something that surprised even me. A stout fellow with a shock of dark hair was climbing down the rope ladder from the ship onto the barge. It must be Romero. The man had nerve; I'll say that for him.

I could now see the events clearly through the binoculars as the lights from the ship were illuminating the scene. Romero was now on deck and turned to face Frankland. He moved over to him and in a warm gesture gave him a hug. Frankland was seemingly delighted by this. After all, it was his moment of triumph, defying the odds and bringing the barge of explosives to him.

But, then, something occurred that seemed wrong. Frankland started to slump and fell out of Romero's arms onto the deck. It was then I could see what had happened. Romero had not just been embracing him, but sticking a knife into his back. Kicking the man's body to one side, he then went over to Elisa and cut through the bonds that held her to the mast. Houghton watched all this from the helm, impervious to the action. Without much ado Romero put his arm around Elisa and dragged her towards the rope ladder. After a few words she seemed persuaded to climb it. Romero followed immediately behind pushing her if she slowed, cajoling her to keep climbing. They were soon on the ship, with Elisa being helped over the rail and onto the deck.

Meanwhile below them on the deck of the barge Houghton was checking the body of Frankland. He then got on his knees to inspect the device that the madman had been threatening to blow them up with. Suddenly, as if inspired by a dervish, he sprang to his feet and shouted something up towards the captain of the *Plate*, who was standing on the bridge of the ship above him. What it was, I could not hear, but it seemed like a warning of some kind.

Within seconds the crew of the *Plate* were pulling in the rope ladder and cargo nets. I could see Romero shouting at the bridge gesturing to make the captain accelerate the ship forward and away from the barge.

Almost concurrently with this, Houghton left the body, and stepped onto the rail of the barge. With great aplomb he then dived elegantly into the cold estuary waters. The ship was now already beginning to pull away, heading due north.

I gestured to Jack to try and get us closer to Houghton, who was about a furlong distance and swimming strongly.

We were halfway between ourselves and him when it happened. The barge exploded. A massive blast that sent debris into the air some distance. We all ducked down, and put our hands over our heads to protect us from the flying wood splinters. The sound had made my ears ring out of control. After a few seconds I looked back. The barge had disappeared, just disintegrated. Beyond it, still steaming powerfully away was the *River Plate*, seemingly undamaged. The wash from the explosion rocked our boat back and forth so violently I thought we might sink. But it survived. So did Houghton. Seemingly unruffled by his pride and joy being turned to dust he had continued swimming and was soon being helped on board our yawl. He was cold, wet, exhausted but remarkably alive and unharmed. We sat him up in the boat. Oddly, none of us could speak for some time. We just stared at each other, incredulous as to what had just occurred. I gave him my coat to warm him up.

Jack expertly brought our craft back into harbour grateful that we had survived the explosion.

Back on the quay we were greeted by the harbourmaster and an entourage of officials. Houghton and Audsley were re-united and our brave but wet hero was soon swaddled in a thick blanket and sipping from a mug of cocoa. The three of us were taken into the harbourmaster's office for a debrief. I was loath to say too much and Jack followed my example, Jamie said even less. What had occurred was clearly a shock to everyone. We told as best we could the background story, leaving out our find of Pedro's body at the fort. The harbourmaster seemed out of his depth as we relayed the intricacies of the case. Suffice to say that after an hour it was clear which way the wind was blowing. The explosion on the barge would be reported to the press as a freak accident which sadly claimed the life of an ex officer of the Royal Engineers. Given the royal connection to the Congo survey, and the *River Plate's* role in this, it was best that their efforts to tow the barge out to sea were forgotten. Also, as the ship was well beyond the three-mile limit, and presumably now half way across the Channel, there was no point in trying to intercept her.

By nine o'clock the interview had ended. Houghton and Audsley would be kept in custody overnight and probably charged with offences relating to the carriage of explosives. We were free to depart. That was on the condition that I went to Scotland Yard tomorrow to give a fuller explanation to Detective Sullivan.

At that, myself and Jamie caught the train from Sheerness station, conveniently situated a stone's throw from the office, back to London. Jack would overnight in Sheerness, and take the yawl back to Stanford Creek tomorrow.

This all went accordingly. I took Jamie back to my rooms in Whitechapel where he could sleep in the spare room. He was clearly in a state of shock, whether because of the explosions or seeing the dead Argentinean, I could not fathom.

It had been one hell of a day. I was torn by conflicting feelings; on the one hand we had survived unscathed and had witnessed the death of a thoroughly bad man, Frankland. On the other hand it felt as if Romero had won. He had escaped justice and was heading back to the Argentine with my precious Elisa on board. I could not help but think the unthinkable. Would he push himself on her? Would she feel under so much pressure that she would give in and become his mistress? The very thought made me almost physically retch. No this was not all over; a setback for sure, but not over by a long way.

THIRTY-SEVEN

Scotland Yard 28th September, Morning

IN THE MORNING I TOOK a cab all the way to Scotland Yard, dropping off Jamie at Fenchurch Street so he could get the train home. I was now concerned that Jamie should never have been involved. The whole episode seemed to have traumatised him.

Walking into Sullivan's office at the yard I had a nice surprise. Who was there, bold as brass, but Bill Bannister, sitting across the desk from Sullivan. We shook hands warmly.

"How are you?"

"Good as gold. Bit miffed that I have missed all the excitement." He smiled. It was good to have him back on board. Sullivan was not so enamoured at being ignored.

"Very well, Reeves. I think we've done the handshaking. Now what occurred at Sheerness last night? The telegraph wires have been buzzing for hours."

I sat down and started to put my thoughts together but Bill had other ideas.

"Begging your pardon, Detective, but I have some information which might be of great interest to you."

"Very well, Barrington. What is it?"

"Less than an hour ago, about nine thirty in fact, I got a telegram from an acquaintance in Antwerp. The long and short of it was that the *River Plate* was steaming up the Scheldt towards the city."

I was stunned by this information, and looked at Sullivan. I felt the need to explain further.

"The thing is, after the ship escaped from Sheerness yesterday evening, we assumed it was going straight back to the Argentine, only stopping at the Congo en route. You see, it is not just about Romero getting away with it, he also has Elisa being held hostage on board."

I sat back and looked at the detective. He read my mind.

"So you want to travel to Antwerp to see if you can get her back and have Romero arrested?"

"Absolutely."

"I am afraid that will not be possible. We do not have the jurisdiction in Belgium to make arrests."

"That is ridiculous. You do realise that Romero knifed Frankland, killed him, stone dead. If a murder is not enough for an arrest, then what is?"

Sullivan sat interweaving his fingers.

"I get the impression from the harbourmaster's report that this incident may have occurred outside the three-mile limit. That is, on the high seas, which is not the area where I have jurisdiction. Sorry, I cannot work outside the law. Simple as that."

We sat quietly for a moment, and then Bill interjected. "My guess is that Romero has to make good the explosives lost last night in the barge."

I raised my eyebrows. He continued.

"The story is already in the newspapers this morning. Headline is: *Accident in the Thames estuary. One man killed in explosion.* That is how the story is being told to the public."

I thought for a second or two, and then responded.

"If that is true then he will have to replace the lost explosives in order to fulfil his contract and take them on to the Congo. So he will be buying dynamite in Antwerp, as quick as you like, then loading them onto his ship. Obviously it will not be as profitable as using the stolen explosives that Frankland was bringing him, but a contract is a contract."

Sullivan looked at his hands again.

"Normally I would have you questioned at length about this whole affair, Reeves, but I trust you to give me a full and honest statement, when required. So, I assume you gentlemen will be going to foreign climes to sample the world famous Belgian ales, or whatever. Am I correct?"

"Indeed," I replied.

Sullivan stood up; it was time for us to leave.

"Then, good luck, and be on your way."

THIRTY-EIGHT

Boat and Train to Belgium, 29th September, Morning

THE NEXT MORNING I ARRIVED at Charing Cross at sunrise to get the first train down to the Dover boat train. I had prepared as much as possible – telegramming Edward Hope to let him know my plan of action. Bill had also contacted his friend in Antwerp who had booked a hotel and would meet me on arrival. All was set fair. The main problem was that I had no idea what to do when I got there. There were no powers to arrest Romero and if he chose to stay on board his ship, there was precious little chance of even meeting him. As for Elisa, she was probably being kept below deck in a cabin without even a porthole. Notwithstanding all that, if there was a one in a hundred chance of saving Elisa, I had to try it.

By late morning I had arrived in Calais and then by early afternoon, after a change of trains, was at Antwerp central station. I was staying at the railway hotel so only had to walk a short distance. I was pleasantly surprised by the look of Antwerp and the quality of its architecture and its obvious wealth. It did not surprise me at all that the king, and no doubt local businessmen, were happy to invest in expeditions to open up the Congo for trade.

The hotel was a splendid affair. I walked into the reception area and was pleasantly surprised by the height of the ceiling, the ornate decoration, and magnificent chandeliers. No sooner had I set foot in the place when a well-dressed gentleman approached me.

"Hello, Oliver Rochelle." He thrust his hand forward and gave a warm handshake. His English was immaculate though with a slight French accent.

There were smiles all around.

"William Reeves at your service."

"On the contrary, it is I who will be serving you."

We sat down on the fine leather armchairs that decorated the reception and he opened the conversation.

"Now, I think you want to get straight down to business. Am I right?"

"Indeed."

"Well I think you are in luck. The *River Plate* is now berthed in the southern docks about a mile upstream from here. I believe it is waiting to load some consignments of explosives. Am I right?"

I nodded.

"So we know where the ship will be tonight. Loading will not be finished until late Monday, probably Tuesday morning departure. Not much happens today in Antwerp, it being Sunday, so I expect Romero will stay on board the ship. Probably it is best for you to settle in and we can reconvene tomorrow."

THIRTY-NINE

Antwerp, Café Belgique, 30th September

I MET OLIVER THE NEXT morning. He was bright eyed and bushy tailed. "I have some news for you. It seems Romero has disembarked and is in the city himself."

My ears pricked up at this.

"Do you know where he is?"

"I can guess where he will be later, not half a kilometre from where we are now, in the Café Belgique, just past the cathedral on the main street. No doubt eating and drinking his fill."

I could hardly believe Romero's audacity.

"The man has got some front after all he has done."

Oliver nodded.

"The man has an inflated sense of his own importance. Because the Congo survey is promoted by King Leopold, he feels totally safe being onshore and eating at the finest Antwerp restaurants."

I concurred.

"Perhaps his arrogance will be his undoing. Let us go to this café now and see what he has to say for himself."

Just as we were making ready to depart the hotel manager came over and introduced himself. On ascertaining that I was William Reeves, he handed me a telegram. I read it quickly.

"It's from Edward Hope; he is coming over to Antwerp immediately and bringing Jamie with him."

I was slightly surprised at this. Oliver looked at me quizzically.

"What is the matter William?"

"Edward Hope is coming over but he is also bringing Jamie with him. I don't know if that's wise."

For the rest of the morning Oliver showed me some of the sights of the city but in truth my only desire was to come face to face with Romero again. Finally shortly after twelve we set out for the restaurant. We strode down the main street with my host pointing out numerous facts about the fine architecture on show. That was what had probably lured Romero to do business here, the place smelt of money. The man was no fool.

Within minutes we were standing outside the restaurant. It did not take long to spot our quarry, seated at a good table near the window were Romero and another fellow with Latin features, presumably the ship's captain. It was clearly a fine-dining establishment as the table had spotless white linen and silver cutlery. I felt no desire to hold back so immediately walked into the restaurant and over to his table, pulled out a chair for myself and one for Oliver, and sat down facing the pair.

Surprisingly Romero seemed unfazed. He spoke first, in measured tones.

"Well, if it isn't Mr Reeves and… I don't think I have had the pleasure."

My Belgian host spoke up.

"Oliver Rochelle, shipping agent."

Romero took this information in and glanced at his dining companion before continuing. "So, to what do we owe this pleasure?"

I looked at him in the eye. His brimming self-confidence was perplexing and unsettling.

"And this gentleman is the captain of the *River Plate* Ricardo Fernandez."

Fernandez proffered a handshake but we refused.

"Now, Mr Reeves, I hope there will be no nastiness involved. I am assuming that you are both unarmed and merely wish to speak to me?"

I nodded.

"So, carry on. How can I help you?"

I breathed in deeply.

"Quite simply I wish you to release Elisa Pound, who, I believe, is a prisoner on your ship. No more, no less."

"Why would she want to leave the ship? To be taken by you back to England, I don't think so. You see the truth is that she is enjoying the voyage and looking forward to the warmer climes in Africa and South America. She is already settled into her luxury cabin and being well fed and cared for. What have you got to offer her that I have not?"

His arrogance was galling me.

"I am trying to be reasonable here. I know you murdered Frankland and have been involved in numerous other deaths, but I am willing to leave those matters to the police. I merely wish Elisa to come back with me to England. I think it is a fair exchange."

He laughed.

"Mr Reeves, you are somewhat pathetic. A middle-aged failed detective with precious little money. What can you offer her?"

He took a deep slug of the red wine in front of him, wiped his mouth with the napkin, and then continued.

"Whilst I can offer her everything. And I mean everything... You see we Argentineans are not just great businessmen. We are also great lovers. Did it not occur to you that your virginal Miss Pound would rather be... what shall I say, to put it bluntly, fucked, by a gaucho bull, rather than a weakling like yourself?"

The table went awkwardly silent.

"I am sorry to say these things in front of your friend Mr Rochelle here but you English are notoriously bad lovers."

He continued unabashed.

"In fact when I have finished eating and drinking my fill here, I will go back to the boat, to her cabin. She will be happy to see me and delighted that I wish to plant my seed inside her. Is that not right Captain Fernandez?"

"Indeed," he said.

I tried to keep cool but had to say my piece.

"I do not believe a word of that. Elisa would never allow herself to become your mistress. She is better than that. Better than you."

"Dear Mr Reeves, you do not understand the female species. Admittedly she was a little shocked when I pulled her up onto the ship from that awful barge. But when it blew up, an unfortunate accident that killed Mr Frankland, she realised how much she owed me. Then after a good meal, with some fine wines, she was perfectly content to become my mistress again."

I was choking inside but trying to stay calm. Romero was enjoying this, so carried on.

"I say again, advisedly, when she first came to London, into my employ, there were various tasks she had to perform for me. Surely you realised that."

"You're a liar. A lying bastard."

"I think, Mr Reeves, that you are allowing emotion to cloud your judgement. What have you to offer me, or Elisa, for that matter? Nothing."

I was feeling deflated but trying not to let it show.

"Whilst I, Alfonso Romero, am employed in doing important work for King Leopold and am feted here in Antwerp, respected. I can walk down the streets and am highly regarded by the local tradesmen. Eat wherever I like. Perhaps even sample the delights of the young Antwerp ladies of the night. All with impunity, is that not true, Ricardo?"

He nodded.

"And as for your laughable English police, your boys from Scotland Yard, they would not touch me here in a foreign country. So, I will bid you good day."

At that he threw some notes onto the tablecloth, nodded to the waiter, then stood up and walked away. At the door he turned around and gave me some more advice.

"And you can tell Mister Edward Hope to stop sending me telegrams. Did you know he had been doing that? I thought not. Offered me sums of money to release Elisa. Pathetic. He used to be the boss, now he is just an old man chasing shadows. I am the man with all the cards in my hand. I bid you good day."

At that he strode out onto the street, closely followed by Fernandez.

I sat for a few moments staring at Oliver. That had not gone well. Romero's self-confidence seemed to knock everything down in front of him, including me. Finally Oliver spoke.

"Don't believe a word he says. From what Bill has told me about the background to this, there is no way that Elisa has become his mistress. She will be desperate to get off that ship and back to England. We just have to find a way to make it happen."

We sat in silence. I broke it with my thoughts.

"I think he is lying, But we cannot be sure. Romero is so arrogant he thinks he is untouchable and is happy to rub our noses in it."

"Exactly."

"So what is our plan of action, Oliver?"

We sat for a few moments, we were both struggling. Oliver spread his hands in a gesture of hopelessness.

We left the restaurant, both of us feeling a little flattened by what had occurred, and headed back to the hotel. No sooner had we walked through the door when I caught sight of Edward Hope, Bill and Jamie Baldwin, sitting drinking coffee. It was an odd sight. Jamie looked as if he would be far more comfortable in the servants' quarters. Hope spoke up.

"Good to see you, Reeves. I knew you were coming here so had to follow on. See if we can help."

I nodded and gestured towards Jamie, who was still looking ill at ease.

"Brought Bill along as well and Jamie along to carry my bags. He has never been abroad before so I thought it would be a good experience for him."

Jamie piped up. "Never been out of Essex before, sir. Never been in a hotel. This building, it is beautiful. Never seen anything like it, all that decoration. All that brass work."

Bill smiled.

"And I have heard the Belgian beers are worth sampling."

Edward decided the small talk had gone on long enough.

"Well, make yourself useful then, Jamie. Here is the key, take the bags up to the rooms."

Jamie stood up quickly and gathered the bags. The hotel porters were looking on disgruntled. Edward proffered some advice to him.

"Ignore the porters. They just want fat tips. See you back here in a minute."

No sooner had he left the reception than I turned to Edward.

"What is going on? You know Elisa is his mother. The last thing I need is emotions clouding our actions."

"Problem is, Reeves, the cat is out of the bag. I don't know why, but Matilda suddenly decided to tell Jamie the truth, the complete truth. I could not stop her."

"So he knows?"

"You see Matilda did all the donkey work years ago. Romero was still my business colleague then. He told me that Rosina, or Elisa as we now call her, was going off her head. Was not a good mother, could not cope with a position in his company and looking after a young child. Was heading for the lunatic asylums. Could I help? I spoke to Matilda who took the boy and passed him over to Mr and Mrs Baldwin, who desperately wanted a child, and a son at that. I paid them a good allowance as well. It was only after I fell out with Romero that I began to distrust everything that I had been told. But by then it was too late. Frederico had become James, and felt very much part of his new family. He was only four so cannot remember life outside the blacksmith's. So I just let sleeping dogs lie. The same for Matilda."

His voice trailed off. I then chose my words carefully. "We are at a loss as to what to do. Romero seems to have all the cards in his hand. Full support of the Belgian authorities. His ship is leaving tomorrow and I have no idea how to stop it."

At this moment Oliver stepped in.

"I have an idea. It is audacious and I would need to use the services of Bill and the boy Jamie. Is that possible?"

I looked at Hope, we both said yes together.

"Very well, so this is my plan…"

Oliver then went through his idea at length. After ten minutes we all sat back. For some reason we all seemed to look to Hope as being the wise old head of our group. For a moment I thought Hope would tell us we were being ridiculous but instead he wholeheartedly agreed.

Almost on cue, Jamie returned, sans bags.

I smiled. Hope turned to Jamie.

"We have a plan to rescue your mother from Romero's ship. William will run through the details of the plan. Then you will have to tell us if you are willing to take part."

Jamie piped up. "Whatever it is sir. I agree. I would do anything."

I then ran through the plan. At the end there were no questions. Everyone was on board. Which is where I hoped Jamie could be next day.

Hope smiled.

"Very well, we are all organised. Shall we dine here tonight?"

We drifted off to our rooms.

The final act of the day was the evening meal. We sat slightly awkwardly, the four of us. Jamie was enthralled by the chandeliers, the cutlery and crockery and tablecloths and waiters and everything. He had never eaten in a restaurant before. Never drank coffee. The menu was in French, which Oliver kindly translated for us. We had to persuade Jamie that chevaliers were horsemeat, so best avoided. He was also taken aback that the prices were in francs.

The waiters were a little snooty and were probably perplexed by three gentlemen dining alongside a working-class boy, but they were happy when I tipped them generously.

Sleep that night was hard to come by. My mind was racing. At least one way or another tomorrow would be decisive. I looked at the clock, it was past midnight. Today was the day.

FORTY

On the *River Plate*, 30th September, Evening

ON THE CAPTAIN'S TABLE ON the *River Plate* sat Romero, Captain Fernandez and Elisa. Romero was in ebullient form and Elisa's scornful silence only made him louder and more offensive.

"You see what sort of life I have in store for you. The finest foods cooked by the greatest chefs. And this is just the beginning; when we reach the Argentine I will take you to my hacienda, and you will live like a queen."

Elisa did not look up. She was clearly at the table under sufferance.

"I look after my favourite people, is that not right Ricardo?"

"Indeed, sir, it is."

"So that is the future I am offering you… or I can leave you chained up like a dog in one of the cabins at the bottom of the ship until we reach Buenos Aires. It is up to you."

Still silence.

"Or, alternatively, I will throw you off the ship when we reach the Congo. I will leave you on the foreshore. I am sure the Negroes will take you to their hearts. Or perhaps, if you're lucky, you might find a devout missionary, and you can become his wife. You have the pious face suitable for that sort of work."

He threw the napkin onto the table and stood up.

"I have had enough of all this. Tomorrow morning we sail, and it will be the last time you ever see Europe. If you look through your porthole you will see the crowds who will be celebrating our mission to the Congo. Then if you are lucky you might even catch a glimpse of your friend, Mr William Reeves…"

She looked up, surprised by his name being spoken.

"Yes, Mr Reeves. We met him in the city yesterday. He joined us for lunch, all very cordial. He was there with some local fellow, Oliver something or other. They thought they could persuade me to give you up. Just like that."

He stood staring down at her, waiting for some kind of response. He got none.

"So I am sure he will find his way to being on the quayside tomorrow morning. He can take one last look at this boat disappearing into the sunshine, and know he will never see you again." He smirked. Elisa spat on the table.

"You are a very naughty girl. If your behaviour does not improve I will take you to a cabin in the bowels of the ship where having a porthole is just a dream. Your choice."

Elisa looked up. "Why? Why do you hate me so much?"

"Hate, love. Two sides of the same coin. Back home I

think your hate will turn to love once again. We are fated to be together."

He left the dining room. The captain led Elisa back to her cabin. The day was done.

FORTY-ONE

The Departure,
1st October, Morning

Oliver met me for coffee at nine o'clock in the reception. He had good news about the boat's departure.

"I have had it confirmed that the owners, or perhaps it's King Leopold himself, want to make a fuss of the boat leaving for the new Belgium colony of the Congo. So the public will be allowed on the quayside to wave it off, no doubt there will be a brass band as well, and the press. This will play nicely along with our plan."

I was pleased; soon Hope and Jamie appeared and sat down at our table. Jamie had to be persuaded to sit down as he seemed awkward with people a great deal older than himself and in all honesty, of a different social class. We drank tea as this seemed to make Jamie more comfortable. Oliver continued to give us facts about the day to come.

"I will be dressing up for this ruse, and alongside myself on the quay will be Bill. You see, I realised we had one thing missing from this little piece of theatre, we needed an overweight businessman who had clearly spent his life eating and drinking his full. Where could I find such a person? Then Bill came to mind."

Bill gave him a mock slap round the face. Oliver was delighted.

"I will take you up to my office and you can get changed into something more appropriate for your role. The tide is around eleven o'clock this morning and that is the time I am told that they hope to have finished loading and will depart. We must arrive on the quayside around 10.30. I have already arranged for our introduction to the ship's captain."

We arrived at the dock just after ten o'clock. It was a warm morning with the sun rising in the sky. A fine day for a ship leaving port on an adventure to an undiscovered foreign land. I and Edward would be onlookers. Unfortunately our faces were too well known to Romero. It would be Oliver, Bill and Jamie who would have to bring the plan to fruition.

A small crowd was beginning to form. The dock gates were opened and people streamed in. I noticed a brass band arriving with their heavy instrument cases, so gestured for us to follow them in the hope that people would assume we were there as spectators.

We took up a position, close to the quayside, facing the port side of the ship whose bow was heading downriver. There was an air of expectancy. Somebody had put up bunting. Clearly this was an event. The *Plate* was already making steam and it appeared that the loading had been completed.

The brass band had started to play. They were all immaculately dressed in their musicians' uniforms and all seemed to have greased hair and neat black moustaches. I could see the sailors on board doing final safety checks, presumably before withdrawing the gangplank onto the boat.

It was at that moment that our Trojan horse, disguised as a trolley of gifts for the voyage, appeared on the quay. I could see Oliver and Bill, both in full dress: frock coats, cravats and top hats, strutting imperiously alongside a trolley that was being pushed by some local dock workers.

The trolley was a heavy affair, a four-wheeled type with a huge basket of gifts covering the top. There were fruits and chocolates and cigars and everything you can think of. I knew, but hopefully nobody else did, that underneath these gifts was Jamie, tucked up in a ball inside a large basket. Invisible to the naked eye. The plan was for him to get on board undetected, somehow find Elisa's cabin and rescue her. It was a lot to ask.

Oliver and Bill had their role to play in persuading the captain this was all totally genuine. Oliver spoke as we knew Bill's French was poor. He was just to stand there and smile. If challenged, Oliver would explain that he only spoke Walloon. A minor ship's officer had come out to meet them. Oliver spoke loudly with the utmost confidence, laced with some pomposity.

"Let me introduce myself. I am François De Grouyt, Chairman of the Antwerp Chamber of Commerce, my partner here is Andrew Van Dinken, Honorary President of the Chamber of Commerce."

He stood back waiting for the ship's officers to be

impressed. There was precious little of that but they seem to have been taken in by the ruse. Oliver, unabashed, continued.

"On behalf of the Antwerp Chamber of Commerce we would like to present you with these presents to make your journey to Africa more comfortable. We have come here personally to thank you for opening up the Congo for trade."

The ship's officer seemed totally taken in by this. After a few more pleasantries there were handshakes all round and the trolley was pushed up the gangplank onto the ship. Oliver and Bill stood around looking suitably pompous. Some well-meaning locals even went up to thank them and shook their hands. The pantomime had worked.

From within his basket Jamie could hear much of what had been said, although some words were muffled by the cloth which separated him from the gifts above his head. He could feel the trolley moving, then clanking and banging up the gangplank. Another thirty seconds and it had come to a halt. He could hear the men departing who had pushed it onto the boat. The hope was that he would just be left in peace now, as the crew were busy preparing the boat's departure. This seemed to be the case. There was less sound of conversation. Hopefully the trolley had been left unguarded in some obscure part of a corridor. It was brutally warm, curled up in the basket. Within a minute he decided to act and pushed at the weight above him. Inevitably some items crashed onto the floor but his head was instantly out and able to take a deep breath of air. His surroundings were as good as he could hope for. A quiet corridor by the look of it. He gently moved the gifts to one side and placed them quietly on the floor, then took a stride out off the trolley. He looked around again. This time his worst fears were coming true – a crewman stood just feet away staring at him in disbelief. Jamie acted promptly and pulled a knife out of his wristband. In one movement he had covered the few feet to the crewman and pushed the knife to his throat. The man was clearly about to yell but Jamie put a finger to his lips and motioned with the knife. The man knew that one sound, one false move, and he would have had his throat cut. Jamie had learnt a few words of Spanish overnight – the assumption being that the crew would mostly be Argentinean. Though clumsy, the message got through and was something like:

"Take me to the English lady who is locked in a cabin."

The man seemed to understand and nodded. They then set off slowly with the crewman in front and Jamie right behind with the knife discreetly held to his back. For some reason, probably the embarkation rituals, they did not bump into any other crew and were soon in the bowels of the ship. The crewman nodded ahead. Jamie carefully looked around the junction into another corridor that ran at ninety degrees to the one they were on. At the end he could see a man sitting outside a cabin door with what looked like a revolver on his lap. Luckily the man's back was to them.

Jamie gently pulled the crewman back from the junction, then stuffed a wad of material into his mouth and tied up his hands behind him. Jamie had noticed a storeroom a little further back so pushed the crewman into that and wedged the door shut. He then turned around and made his way back to the junction.

The cabin guard was still in the same position, looking bored and not really concentrating on anything other than fiddling with a small pouch of tobacco and some cigarette papers. He was making a roll-your-own cigarette, and this was taking all his attention. Jamie moved swiftly and quietly. Within seconds he was up to the man and had the blade to his throat, scarcely before he had looked up from his cigarette. The knife did the trick. The man was easily persuaded to hand his revolver over to Jamie who then gestured for him to unlock the cabin door. He did so and went in with Jamie right behind him with a gun to his head.

In front of him was what he had longed to see, it was Elisa, scared and confused. She quickly though grasped what was occurring. The guard was pushed into the corner and then made to sit on the bed. Jamie then whisked her into the corridor and locked the cabin door behind him.

"Jamie Baldwin at your service my lady. Mister Hope and Mister Reeves have entrusted me to get you off this boat. So you must follow me."

No sooner had he spoken than the guard started shouting from inside the cabin. Elisa looked at Jamie. He wondered if she had recognised who he was. But there was no time. They scurried along the corridor. Then up a metal staircase to the next deck, then another. Finally they reached the open deck. Luckily it was empty with no crew to be seen. However Jamie was shocked to see that the ship had left the quay and was now heading out into the middle of the river. He could see the fine city of Antwerp now, as a shoreline retreating into the distance. Was it all too late?

Elisa looked at him and spoke. "What are we to do now? It is too late, all too late."

For a moment or two they were both filled with a sense of despair and dread. What could they do?

FORTY-TWO

Back on the Quay

BACK ON THE QUAY I had watched events unfurl. The ruse featuring Oliver and Bill and the Trojan horse had worked well but now events continued unabated. The brass band played their hearts out. The gangplank was pulled in. The crowd shouted and applauded. Dock workers threw the hawsers onto the ship. Within seconds it was edging out from the quay.

Oliver and Bill rejoined us as onlookers. There was no further need for pretence as the ship was now moving towards the centre of the river. My heart was sinking. Even if Jamie was successful in his mission, it might all be too little, too late. Luckily Hope was not one for giving in.

"I have acquired a boat, the small tug over there. If we are quick we can get on board and follow the *River Plate* down the Scheldt."

For once I was disheartened; it now seemed to be desperate.

"What is the point in that? They have nothing between

them now and the North Sea; it's just a straight run down the river into the estuary. We have no chance of getting near her."

Hope was not amused; he was a man of action and authority.

"I have not been idle. The last two days I have besieged the British Embassy here with requests to get the Belgian Excise people to stop the ship leaving the river. It may happen, and if it does, or the ship is held up for any reason, we need to be nearby."

I still felt a sense of helplessness but was grateful for Hope's plan.

"Okay. Let us get on board then without any delay."

At that we quickly walked off the wharf and the dockside to a tugboat moored on a private jetty. It had steam up, and within minutes we were on our way. Clearly Hope, with the local knowledge of Oliver, had a lot of influence around here, or perhaps just a lot of money to grease the palms of the lightermen. My joy about doing something positive was tempered by the fact that the *River Plate* was already in mid-stream making steady progress. This was hopeless. But it felt better to be doing something, than nothing.

FORTY-THREE

Escape from the Ship

JAMIE AND ELISA BOTH LOOKED forlornly towards the riverside frontage of Antwerp. They were too far out now to ever be rescued. It was all hopeless. But Jamie still had the impetuousness of youth. He took the revolver out of his belt and showed it to her.

"I am going to the bridge to force the captain to turn the ship around. I'll put this gun to his head. That should do the trick."

Elisa looked on sadly.

"I know you mean well but there will be too many seamen up there. Even if you get as far as the captain, you'll be overwhelmed. We have to face it, they have won. With this steamship there is no chance of any boat catching us and turning it around."

She looked overwhelmed by sadness. Jamie knew he must rise to the challenge. His eyes went to the funnel and noted the smoke belching out, the powerhouse of the ship.

"So I will go down to the engine room and get them to stop the ship. I know how these boats work. If the stokers stop feeding the furnace, then the boiler loses pressure and it will come to a stop."

At that without waiting for a response he put things in train.

"Get under the canvas. Keep hidden until I come back."

Jamie gestured for her to crawl under a canvas below a lifeboat. She should be undetectable if she stayed still. With that he left her and swiftly made his way down the iron stairs from deck to deck trying to find the ship's engine room.

It did not take too long. He could soon hear the noises of the ship's engineers and the stokers feeding the furnace with coal. He opened the door of the engine room and took his gun out.

It was pretty much what he expected to see. Piles of coal, men working to keep the boiler pressure up by shovelling it into the greedy furnace, smoke and fumes everywhere. The room was hot, acrid and in its centre stood a man who looked as if he might be the chief engineer. His uniform made him stand out from the rest of the stokers and his dirty and sweaty appearance was a sure sign he spent most of his time in the engine room. Behind him were some gauges, possibly the pressure gauge and safety valve.

Jamie raised his gun and pointed it directly at the man.

"Shut off the engines. Bring the boat to a stop. Now!"

The chief engineer looked back at him with a look of total contempt. The stokers stopped shovelling and raised their spades to shoulder height waiting for the order to attack the young upstart.

The chief engineer said something in Spanish. Jamie

knew not what. He then smiled and nodded to the stokers, a sign it seemed that they should quickly and violently deal with Jamie. He had seen enough. Jamie squeezed the trigger. He was not that used to handling guns, in fact this was the first time he had used a revolver.

The shot went wide of the man and hit one of the gauges. The engineer now looked worried. The stokers stopped moving forward. The atmosphere was now incredibly tense as everyone seemed to be waiting to be told what to do next. Jamie could not stop now. He let off another bullet which this time smashed into the boiler behind the engineer. Almost immediately a hiss of boiling steam shot out, almost singeing that engineer. A look of total panic now seemed to affect everyone in the engine room. The hole in the boiler seemed to be enlarging and the steam became more violent and noisy. All the stokers headed for the door throwing their spades to one side. The engineer looked at Jamie in bewilderment then at the gaping hole in the boiler. Within seconds the inevitable happened. The boiler blew! Jamie turned to get away but in less than a second a shaft of boiling water and steam hit the side of his face. The engineer seemed to get the full blast and was writhing in agony on the floor. Jamie was blinded in one eye. He was in shock but knew he had to get out; the gun had dropped out of his fingers. He didn't need it anymore. He was just able to make his way to the door, stumbling over the stokers who were now lying prostrate and clearly in great pain. They had been hit by the full force of steam and boiling water. Jamie looked down at his right arm. The clothes had gone mostly and his skin was red raw In places. Pain was starting to engulf him. He desperately sought a way back to where his mother was.

The ship was now full of smoke and steam and the cries of injured and burnt men. It was pandemonium.

He aimed for the stairs and gradually, painfully, worked his way up inside the boat until finally a blast of fresh air told him that he was back on deck. Somehow, like a wounded animal he staggered on and finally caught sight of Elisa still under the lifeboat. She came out and looked at him with total horror.

"What have you done? You poor boy. What have you done to yourself?"

Jamie could not speak but looked around at the ship's funnel. The smoke coming out of it was now less than before, and a different colour and the boat was clearly slowing down. He looked out onto the river and could see a tugboat moving towards them. He was now in something of a trance such was the shock of the blast and the burns. He pointed to the tugboat. She looked at it. This was all like a strange dream now. Alongside the lifeboat, that she had been hiding under, was a length of rope. Jamie summoned the last of his strength, picked it up and tied one end to the ship's rail. He gestured for her to get onto the rope and climb down the side of the boat. Elisa looked at him in despair, then over her shoulder at the tugboat getting closer. Finally Jamie was able to say a few words through his pain.

"You go first. Get on the boat."

She looked forlornly at him. She could see that death was not long coming as his burns looked too bad, too deep.

"I cannot leave you. Not like this."

Jamie almost cried but finally through his anguish said a few more words.

"Please, Mother. Please go."

She looked at him in disbelief. Was he now completely disorientated and removed from reality? Then she looked a little closer. Despite his burns she could see the resemblance in the face. There was something of him that reminded her of Frederico. At that moment she froze, and stared into his eyes.

"It is you, Frederico…"

He smiled back at her.

"Yes."

She stumbled for the right words.

"After all these years!"

She reached out and gently snuggled his body to hers, and kissed his forehead.

"My poor boy."

Jamie moved away a little so he could speak.

"Why did you leave me?"

"I never did. It was Romero, he told me I was a bad mother and you would be going to better parents in the Argentine. I would never have left you. Never."

Jamie swayed slightly; he was struggling to hear, struggling to stand.

For a few moments they stood looking into each other's eyes. Both were desperate to protect the other but clueless as to how to do this.

Then something happened to break the atmosphere. Behind Jamie, striding along the deck was Romero with a raised pistol. Jamie turned to him but Romero spoke first.

"You. You have half killed my chief engineer and wrecked the boat."

He pointed the gun at Jamie but immediately Elisa leapt in, coming between him and Romero.

"Get out of the way you silly woman. Go back to your cabin while I deal with him!"

She did not move. Romero, convulsed with anger, stepped forward and tried to drag her out of the way with his strong left arm, while keeping his pistol aimed at Jamie. She screamed. Jamie seizing his chance went for Romero's right hand and grabbed the wrist. Using the last of his strength he dragged Romero onto the ground, his hands firmly clasped around Romero's gun hand. Jamie shouted at her.

"Go, go! Down the rope. The tugboat will pull you out of the water."

She hesitated.

He shouted again.

"Go, go!"

At this she did what he wanted and started climbing over the ship's rails.

How Jamie had found the strength to hold Romero's arm down on the cold iron deck, he did not know. But somehow he had done it. Romero was furious, like a trapped animal, and kept pushing with his left hand to get him off. The revolver had now come loose from his fingers and Jamie had kicked it along the deck. Romero stared into his eyes and redoubled his efforts to push him off. He was a strong man, far bigger than Jamie. There was only going to be one winner.

Just as Jamie's strength was failing him, he heard a shriek and a loud splash of water. She must have fallen into the river. He knew he must follow, and rescue her if needed.

Suddenly he let go of Romero and headed for the guardrail. Without pausing and before Romero could regain control of his revolver, Jamie was over the side and hurtling towards the river below, feet first.

The Scheldt was bitterly cold, even on this mild day. When he hit the water all the air was blown out of his lungs. Panic set in. He took in a mouthful of river water then bobbed up and down, frantically trying to take in a breath. He was in shock with the cold, the brutal icy cold, and the feeling of pressure on his lungs.

I saw all this from the tugboat. Elisa had fallen from the rope, heavily into the water, and was now floating with the tide. I was frozen in disbelief. Seconds later, a man who I knew must be Jamie jumped from the ship, feet first into the water. I could not hesitate any longer. I knew what I should do. Without thought I climbed over the tug's handrail and jumped into the river. The shock on hitting the water was enormous. All the breath was knocked out of me and the cold made it almost impossible not to panic. My head bobbed up so I could take some painful breaths of fresh air. But soon, almost imperceptibly my body grew accustomed to the freezing water. Without more hesitation I set off in the direction of Elisa. It was a desperate breast stroke, I was moving in her direction but everything seemed in slow motion. I was a swimmer but not a particularly strong one. But then just as all seemed lost, I could see her right in front of me. I reached out and somehow got my arms underneath her shoulders, keeping her head above water. She seemed dead to the world. I was desperately trying to stay afloat, treading water as best I could. But it felt hopeless. Then miraculously another head appeared. It was Jamie. He was swimming strongly. Together we somehow manhandled Elisa back towards the tug. Even then I doubted we would make it. I cursed my lack of strength, my incompetence as a swimmer but just as all seemed lost, an iron grappling hook came out from somewhere. I grabbed at it and tucked it under my right arm while still gripping Elisa with my left. Even though she was a complete deadweight, she was somehow pulled out off the water into that boat. She was followed by myself and then Jamie. Somehow, in some way, the crew of the tugboat got us into the boat. The lightermen had done a fantastic job; we all owed our lives to them.

I was laid out on deck and turned to one side to spit out any water. She was laid out on the deck alongside me. Jamie seemed to be the only one of us still sitting upright. The lad must be strong as an ox but oh, my god, what bad burn injuries he had. So much of his skin was red raw and starting to blister. I could see Bill, Oliver and Hope, looking down at us, desperate to see if we would be alright.

Above our tugboat, but now moving away, was the *River Plate*, and standing by the ship's guardrail was Romero. For a second or two, he looked down, then with a scornful shrug, moved away out of sight.

Hope was taking her pulse. It was obviously weak, very weak. She was put onto her side in the hope that any river water would come out. A little did, but nothing more. No sign of life.

They gently tugged her hair off her face and then wrapped her in a warming blanket. I was slightly better and was able to just about sit with my back to the handrail, also wrapped in something warm.

The tug raced back to the quay and signalled ahead that an ambulance was needed. Within a few minutes they were lifting her prostrate body onto a stretcher then into an ambulance. Jamie followed her into the ambulance, thankfully still walking. For a moment I lost it.

"Please, Elisa, please wake up. We all love you. Please."

Then the doors of the ambulance were closed. I travelled in another ambulance to the main hospital in Antwerp accompanied by Bill and Hope. Here she was taken into the ward and doctors started working on her, trying to find out why she would not awaken. I was also treated for the cold and after some mugs of hot cocoa soon felt better. Jamie was receiving a lot of treatment for his burns and was soon swathed in bandages. Nevertheless, despite his ordeal, and his burns, he still seemed in good spirits. I stayed at the hospital. Finally after a long wait I was called in and told that it looked as if Elisa's skull had been fractured, or at least badly bruised, in the fall into the river and that this accounted for her unconscious state.

We steeled ourselves for the wait for her to regain consciousness.

FORTY-FOUR

Epilogue

Days passed. Elisa was still unconscious, in a coma. Meanwhile Hope had accompanied Jamie back home to England. He was still unwell and covered in bandages from his ordeal but deemed well enough to travel. Oliver had pushed the Belgian police to investigate what had occurred on the ship. With Elisa unable to be interviewed, the story to the police was told by Romero. He stated that Jamie had gone mad, had gone into the boiler room and caused the serious injury of the chief engineer by damaging the ship's boiler. When he had then cornered him on deck, Jamie had pulled a gun on him. He had no choice but to apprehend him. Then both Jamie and Elisa had chosen to jump overboard. All his actions were acts of self-defence. Oliver did not believe it, neither did I, but it seemed to be what the local police wanted to hear. There could be an inquest into what had occurred, and it was possible that Jamie might be brought back to explain his actions. However as cross examining Jamie might lead to the whole story of Elisa's kidnap being revealed, the chances were that Romero would press for any charges against Jamie to be quietly dropped.

Every day I visited Elisa in hospital, but frustratingly there was no change in her condition. She was still dead to the world.

On the fourth day Oliver came to see me, sitting alongside her in the hospital ward.

"I have some news for you William. Romero has not left the city yet. His boat is now in the graving dock on the east side of the river, no doubt having a new boiler installed. And, he is there, no doubt supervising the work."

That was all I needed to know.

"Thank you Oliver. I think I will pay him a visit. A courtesy call you might call it."

Oliver looked worried.

"Don't do anything rash."

I smiled and headed for the hospital entrance. In thirty minutes I had crossed the river and arrived at the graving dock. I could immediately see the *River Plate* sitting within the waterless dry dock, whilst workmen flustered around her. To my astonishment, he was there. Romero in person. Strutting along the dockside, staring down into the deep dock and shouting at hapless workmen. I took my chance. The graving dock had no perimeter wall so all I needed to do was walk with confidence, as if I was part of the harbour management perhaps, towards him. He didn't see me for a while, and I was perhaps less than twenty foot distant, when he looked at me and spoke.

"Mister Reeves. To what do I owe this pleasure?"

I did not hesitate.

I lunged at him pushing him off his feet and onto the ground. He now looked nervously towards the edge of the walkway, just a few feet distant from the steep, vertical, drop into the dry dock. I could no longer contain my rage.

"You bastard. You have probably killed Elisa!"

He swore and clawed and bit me. His workers looked on, clearly wondering if, or how, they should intervene. But then fate stepped in. Somehow, we had both pushed in the same direction, and like some sort of deranged beer barrel were rolling towards the edge of the dock.

Then, all was frozen in time. Still in a clinch but seemingly far slower than in real life, we fell into the dock.

By sheer chance, when we hit the concrete floor, Romero was underneath me. The impact was incredible. Every ounce of air was sucked out of my lungs, every part of my body was hurting, and my ribs were probably gone, broken. I stared into the sky, desperate not to lose consciousness. From way above, faces looked down at me. Pain was everywhere. Never ending. Finally I managed to breathe in the tiniest morsel of air. Even that was hideously painful. I seemed to be alive… just.

I looked at Romero. He was lying alongside me. There was no movement. Blood was coming out of his head, colouring his dark curly hair, red. It looked like his skull was fractured. I lay there supine. Time had no meaning. Then some men came and put me onto a stretcher, I was passing out with the pain. I caught one last glance at him. He had not moved one iota. The crowd of workmen just looked down on him. Perhaps justice had been finally done.